SHORT STORIES

from the pages of the *TLS*

Edited by Lindsay Duguid

CONTENTS

FOREWORD

FOREWORD

The shock of short fiction – the sense of being suddenly removed to another place – works strongly within a context of contrasts. Readers coming on a single story in the serious pages of the *New Statesman* or the *New Yorker* will register the change of tone and realize that they are about to be let off the hook and allowed to plunge into elemental material. The sixteen stories here, which appeared in the *TLS* at intervals over fourteen years but mainly between 1988 and 2000, provided a break from the judicious assessment going on in the other pages. They offered exercise for the imagination, rhythms and echoes for the alert ear and a glimpse of another – often weirder – world.

The length of the stories – 4,000 words was the limit set, two and a half *TLS* pages – means that they are exceptionally concise and sharp. There is no room for a leisurely introduction or elaborate scene-setting. Straight away, we are gripped by the paranoid tones of Julian Barnes's concert-goer, by the hostages to fortune sent up like kites by Penelope Fitzgerald's *plein-air* painter, and by Hilary Mantel's direct address to us: "Before you can speak, even before you take your first steps outside your house, there is a moment when you are lost or found." James Lasdun's esoteric gathering in a drawing-room near the North Circular Road and the important party Amit Chaudhuri's Mr and Mrs Gupta are preparing for with some nervousness ("Seven thirty. But eight o'clock would be all right, don't you think?") set us up for events of significance. All of this must be unravelled, the puzzle solved by the story's end.

Writing a story for the *TLS* seems to have encouraged a level of sophistication, an assumption of familiarity with or interest in Shostakovich, installation art, quantum physics. The surfaces of many of the stories here are studded with references to specific areas of knowledge, an awareness of important distinctions to be made in the history of the Irish Civil War, say, or the essential difference between the *Iliad* and the *Odyssey*, the personalities of different breeds of dog. The jokes are sharp and sly. Helen Simpson's two women friends exchange wisdom about handling alcohol: "'Never drink when you're angry, lonely, tired, hungry or bored.' 'So, never', said Holly. 'Basically.

Cheers.'" The first time he sleeps with a woman, Tibor Fischer's narrator learns "why most people would do almost anything for sex, that her interest in him had nothing to do with him, and that everyone gets one free fuck".

Another demand of writing at this length is to create a strong and vivid happening within a short space. Here, the writers achieve lift-off in a small compass, amid some subfusc and shabby settings. John McGahern describes a boy and his father going on steadily planting potatoes in the cold, while not far away, a troop of men with guns wreaks mayhem, and a bullock, accidentally hit, goes "bawling and roaring" round in circles in a field. David Malouf's retired newsagent, shot in cold blood in the middle of the Australian outback, registers on the point of death the stony ground ('They were a surprise those stones. Usually he was careful about them. Bad for the mower"). A lifetime of disappointment goes into Penelope Fitzgerald's red-haired girl, too poor to get hold of the red shawl which will provide colour contrast for the artist who is painting her; and an unwelcome flood of self-knowledge comes to Mr Gupta when he sees himself through the eyes of his boss's young son. The movement from the ordinary to the extraordinary is perhaps parallel to the movement of the reader from the safer world of book reviews to the space of a story where anything can happen.

The way the stories were chosen – with most of them, I asked the writers I admired if they would like to submit something, a handful of others came unsolicited – means that the selection is without an overarching theme, an agenda or a brief to fill. This may be why they seem so fresh and original; various, lively, speaking of their time. We are very pleased to be able to offer such a strong and enjoyable collection and are grateful to the writers who have allowed us to reprint their stories here. "Some Time I Shall Sleep Out", by Julian Maclaren-Ross, was written in 1957 and published for the first time in the *TLS* in December 2002, with the permission of the Harry Ransom Humanities Research Center at the University of Texas at Austin, and the Estate of Julian Maclaren-Ross. Our thanks go to them, and to Paul Willetts, who retrieved the story from obscurity.

LINDSAY DUGUID
January 2003

Babushka in the Blue Bus

By Shena Mackay

The 196 bus is elusive and blue and plies between Norwood and Brixton, painted with advertisements for Italy and the Caribbean, and seems to those who ride in it to have been stamped out of tin or constructed from rusty Meccano. It shudders and judders, the windows rattle in their sockets and are assaulted by branches of chestnut trees. On the afternoon of Good Friday, just about the time when there should have been darkness over all the land, the lower deck of the bus was taken over by a Gospel Choir whose minibus had broken down. Their crimson dresses and blazers packed the seats like a consignment of Papa Meilland roses that had escaped from a garden centre in full bloom, and almost immediately a melodious hum, as if bees were at work among the petals, drifted upstairs and swirled in the cigarette smoke.

Reginald Winchester, not his real name, sitting in the front left-hand seat of the upper deck, turned up his coat collar to protect himself from "When I Survey the Wondrous Cross", the exhalations of righteous roses whose scent pierced him like thorns. The camel-hair was ringed with grease where his thinning plumage rested on it and the buttons hung from shanks of mismatched thread, but that coat had been a star in its time, acting, with a pair of caddish suede shoes now as smooth as leather, its wearer off the screen. His tightly buckled trenchcoat, his Homburg, his Trilby, his gun and his sneer had done their best to edge full black-and-white B-features into film noir, but at most his appearances evoked tired nudges of "It's 'im, whatsisname, you know, that one that was in that film . . . ." Unopened bluebells in a garden blurred his eyes like unripe asparagus bluish with cold, and then, outside a church, a jaundiced poster spiked with a black crown of thorns. "It's all your fault," he muttered, "for nearly two thousand years we've had Sunday licensing laws on a Friday, thanks to you. Bank holidays, who needs them?"

He had a One Day Travelcard in his wallet, and he was travelling to nowhere.

Subliminal tinned asparagus tips brushed his memory and he felt a queasy desire for a Sunday tea of lettuce in a cut-glass bowl, with canned salmon drowning a greenfly in salty water and beetroot tingeing the tinned Vegetable Salad with pink; apricots in Carnation milk and the pink and yellow windowpanes of Battenburg Cake. He had been twenty-two when he had discovered that Battenburg cake was common. He wondered now if he would have been happier if he had never been disabused of the notion that it was posh. He jerked uneasily in his seat, noting and dismissing instantly two young women three or four seats behind him.

Terry was not sure how it had been her fault that they had passed that dead frog on the way to the bus stop, but Holly's white averted profile made it clear that she was to blame. She touched her friend's hand and offered a cigarette, and was answered by a shift of the shoulder.

"Don't be so prickly, Holly."

Holly moved into the seat across the aisle.

"Well, I see this is going to be one of our memorable outings", Terry said to the window, and lit a cigarette. A little breeze sneaked in and blew her smoke across Holly's stricken face. The day had started badly, with Holly faking a stomach-ache to postpone once again the long-promised visit to Terry's family, and when Terry had responded with two aspirin and an effusion on the restorative air of Woodside Park, Holly had waved away her breakfast tray and dressed bitterly in her least becoming clothes, combat fatigues appropriate for a saboteur. She had refused also to eat any lunch. Terry inhaled grey disappointment and imagined shoving her friend's head through the glass; but then how to introduce her to Mummy and Dad . . . . "This is Holly, who I accidentally decapitated on the bus . . . . she's much prettier really, and those trousers don't do her justice . . . ."

"No thank you." Holly, staring through the window, unaware of its violent impact and of her head rolling down the hill, dismissed the plate of sandwiches held out by Terry's mother. A frog squatted on a wholemeal triangle. She shivered. She hated cucumber anyway. She hated Terry's mother, whom she had never met. It had just sat there, dead, pretending to be alive, on the pavement outside the Doctor's, as if it had been about to hop into the surgery, and hadn't made it in time. Terry would have stepped on it if she, Holly, hadn't screamed. Typical of her insensitivity. It was disgusting, and somebody should have cleared it away.

"I've heard so much about you," she said to Terry's brother, "and if I hear one more word I'll throw up."

Teresa and Terence, the twins. Terry and Terry. She really did have a stomach-ache now; dread gripped her like a hungry octopus.

"Oh dear, I am being awkward, aren't I?" she smiled. "I do apologize. I thought Terry would have warned you about my food allergies . . . no, it's only a little scratch, please don't worry."

She pulled up her trouser leg to reveal long reddening welts where the dog's claws had raked her skin. Lambert, the lovable Bedlington terrier, was dragged yowling from the room. She knew that sheepish poseur too well from the snap-shots pinned above Terry's bed.

"I hate you, I hate you, I hate you!"

Terence's four-year-old daughter was on top of her, pounding her with tiny fists. She was smacked too, and put outside the door, her shrieks mingling with the dog's howls.

"You OK, babe? You look quite flushed."

"I told you I wasn't well. I was just thinking about your family."

"It'll be fine, I promise. We'll probably go for a walk after tea – you won't even have to talk to them much. It'll be easy – they're all dying to meet you."

"I've got a blister", she said.

Pushing whiny kids on rusty swings. Lambert, forgiven, pursuing Canada geese across a lake, grinning and shaking droplets of muddy water over her, and everybody laughing. She had detested Canada geese ever since boring wild-life documentaries at school.

"Oh sacred head, sore wounded . . ." swirled up the stairs.

"Jesus wept!" said Holly.

The man in the front seat whirled round to confront her. That was the one blasphemy which he could not countenance. His eye was caught, however, by an old woman lunging from the top step with a heavy shopping-bag. She made her way to the long seat at the back. A warm, spicy smell of cinnamon and yeast and candied peel began to tantalize the noses of her fellow passengers. Reginald's eyes prickled in memory of an Easter garden of primroses and grape hyacinths in damp starry moss and a pebble rolled away from the mouth of a miniature cave. Baby leaves unfurled from fat reddish buds at the window; he took refuge from their freshness in a cigarette.

The tip of Terry's tongue licked her lips, luxuriating in an anticipation of buttery crumbs on a plate wreathed in convolvulus. The juddering of the bus was giving her a slight headache, and she knew from experience that concentrating on food was the best remedy for motion sickness. She saw the amaryllis, white, tipped with palest pink, flaunting against the bay window, the rosewood piano, the hot cross buns, the butter in the green glass dish. She had looked forward for such a long time to taking Holly to her childhood home but now she saw her hopes flushed way in an anorexic excess in the bathroom papered with fading peacocks.

Holly was regretting her rejected breakfast and lunch. "What's that smell?" she demanded. "It reminds me of some-thing . . . ."

Terry looked round. "I think it's coming from that old lady", she whispered.

"The Urals, or the Ukraine", thought Reginald. The bright cotton scarf tied round her high-cheekboned face, the black stockings – she should have held a wicker basket on her lap covered with a snowy napkin, instead of that splitting plastic holdall, and perhaps a drowsy hen clucking reassuringly over a clutch of warm eggs, an aromatic bunch of rough green herbs, a string of dome-shaped onions, black bread and sour red wine.

There was a scuffle and the scrape of claws, panting and swearing, as a dog dragged a boy, on the end of a lead, upstairs, followed by a girl. The humans slumped into a seat and the boy dropped the lead. The dog sashayed down the aisle, jumped on to the long seat at the back and flopped down beside the Babushka, fixed her eyes on the black shopping-bag and started to whine. The greasy dust that filmed every hair made her coat appear to be grey; black dragged nipples were evidence of puppies in her past. A wisp of rainbow chiffon twined in her studded collar was a festive or paschal touch at odds with her hangdog mien. Her whines grew more persistent, and were ignored by the youth with a crooked swastika tattooed on his forehead, and the girl with a draggle of dried blood on her thigh under the torn mesh of her fishnet stocking. Terry was distressed. She thought of Lambert, and how she would have liked to have him to live with her, but the flat was no place for a dog. This was rottweiler and dobermann country. Pit bull territory where dogs were kept as guards and weapons. She turned her head as the old woman succumbed, groped in her bag, and broke off a piece of something and slipped it to the dog. She almost lost her fingers. Then the dog was standing over her, yelping for more.

"Hey", exclaimed the youth, "that dog's eating a hot cross bun!"

Two more pairs of hungry eyes bored into the black bag.

"That's not fair", said the girl.

"What about us then?" the youth accused.

With a smile of defeat or graciousness, the old woman held out a paper bag. They lurched down the bus.

"What about us then?" asked Holly.

"Holly!"

Holly was leaning over the back of the seat extending a hand.

"Mmmm, this is brilliant!" she sighed through crumby teeth. "Home made, and still warm! Terry, you've got to try one!"

Thus commanded by her friend, who seemed to be her friend once more, what could Terry do but sidle sheepishly after her?

"Are you sure you can spare another?" she said, biting into her bun, "if only we had some butter . . . ."

The old woman either could not oblige, or did not understand.

"Mind if I join you?"

Reginald, unable to maintain detachment as the dog embarked on, and swallowed almost whole, a second bun, gave a little bow as he sat down.

"Please."

The Babushka passed the paper bag, now holding one last bun.

The fat kid was right; it bore no resemblance to the cellophane-wrapped objects which, with no sense of occasion and brittle pastry crosses, had stocked the supermarket shelves for weeks. As he chewed, looking out of the window at an ancient cherry tree veiled in heartbreaking white, he had a shaky notion that there might even now be redemption by natural and human agencies.

"Herne Hill, Herne Hill, so good they named it twice . . .", he said.

"Didn't you used to be whatsisname, you know, the one who was in those old films on telly?" asked the boy.

"Not really", replied Reginald.

He half rose, in half-gentlemanly fashion, as the Babushka stood and began to make her way towards the stairs.

"Happy Easter!", called Terry and Holly, to her disappearing headscarf.

Terry looked down and saw her standing on the pavement, a bent black figure engulfed by crimson gospellers, outside a closed supermarket.

"Most unorthodox", mused Reginald. "I thought Russians observed the Julian calendar."

May 5, 1988

Vigilance

By Julian Barnes

It all started when I poked the German. Well, he might have been Austrian as it was Mozart, and it didn't actually start then, it started years before, but you always have to say when things start, don't you? And it wasn't really his fault. Except it was. He knew it. I could see guilt in his face when he turned.

It was a Thursday in November, 7.30 at the Festival Hall, Mozart K595 with Andras Schiff, followed by Shostakovich 4. I remember thinking as I set off that the Shostakovich had some of the loudest passages in the history of music, and you certainly wouldn't be able to hear anything over the top of that. But this is jumping ahead. It was a normal audience, and the hall was virtually full. The last people to arrive were the ones who'd been at the sponsor's pre-concert drinks downstairs. You know the sort – oh, it seems to be about half-past, let's go and have a pee, then wander up to our seats. The boss is putting up some cash, so Maestro Haitink can hang on a bit in the green room.

The Austro-German may have been part of some group or outing. Anyway, he was smallish, baldish, with glasses, a sticky-up collar and bow tie. Not exactly evening dress; perhaps a going-out gear typical of where he came from. And he was pretty bumptious, I thought, not least because he had two women with him, one on either side. They were all in their mid-to-late thirties, I'd say; old enough to know better. "These are good seats", he announced as they found their places: J 37, 38 and 39. I was in K 37, just behind them. I instantly took against him. Praising himself to his escorts for the tickets he'd bought. Well, maybe not. Perhaps he'd got them from an agency, and was just relieved; but he didn't say it like that. And I wasn't in the mood to give him the benefit of the doubt.

As I said, it was a normal audience. Everyone on day release from the city's hospitals, with pulmonary wards and ear-nose-and-throat departments getting ticket priority. Book now for a better seat if you have a cough which comes in at more than 95 decibels. At least people don't fart in concerts. Anyway, I've never heard anyone fart. I expect they do. Which is partly my point: if you can suppress at one end, why not at the other? You get roughly the same amount of warning in my experience. But people don't on the whole fart raucously in Mozart. So I suppose vestiges of the thin crust of civilization which prevents our decline into barbarism are just about holding.

The opening allegro went pretty well: a couple of sneezes, a bad case of compacted phlegm in the middle of the terrace which nearly required surgical intervention, one digital watch and a fair amount of programme-turning. I sometimes think they ought to put directions for use on the cover of programmes. Like: "This is a programme. It tells you about tonight's music. You might like to glance at it before the concert begins. Then you will know what is being played. If you leave it too late, you will cause a certain amount of low-level noise, you will miss some of the music, and risk annoying your neighbours, especially the man in seat K 37." Of course, they enclose some information vaguely bordering on advice. For instance, this: "Coughing. Loud, uncovered coughing during a concert can be very distracting. It will be much appreciated if you would use a handkerchief to reduce the noise." But does anyone pay any heed to this? It's like smokers reading the health warning on a packet of cigarettes: they take it in and yet they don't take it in; at some level, they don't believe it applies to them. It must be the same with the coughers. Not that I want to sound too understanding: that way lies forgiveness. And just on a point of information, have you ever seen anyone at a concert take out a handkerchief to reduce the noise? I've seen it only once. I was at the back of the stalls, T 21. The Bach double concerto. My neighbour, T 20, began rearing up as if athwart a bronco. With his pelvis thrust forward, he hurriedly pulled out his handkerchief, accompanied by a bunch of keys. Their shaming fall distracted him, so that handkerchief and sneeze went off in separate directions. Thank you very much, T 20. Then he spent the rest of the slow movement wondering whether or not he could pick up his keys, eyeing them as if theft were highly probable. Eventually he solved the problem by putting his foot on top of them and smugly returning his gaze to the orchestra. The faint metallic crunch from beneath his shoe added a new sound to my repertoire.

The allegro ended, and Maestro Haitink slowly lowered his head, as if giving everyone permission to use the spittoon and talk about their Christmas shopping. J 39 – the Viennese blonde, a routine programme-shuffler and hair-adjuster, had a lot to say to Mr Sticky-Up Collar in J 38. He was nodding away in agreement, about the price of pullovers or something. Maybe they were discussing Schiff's delicacy of touch. I don't care. Haitink raised his head to indicate that it was time for the chatline to go off air, lifted his stick to demand the end of coughing, then threw in that subtle, cocked-ear half-turn to indicate that he, personally, for one, was now intending to listen very carefully indeed to the pianist's entry. The larghetto, as you probably know, begins with the unsupported piano announcing what those who have bothered to read the programme would know to expect as a "simple, tranquil melody". This is the concerto in which Mozart declined the use of trumpets, clarinets and drums: clearly, without such rivalry, the piano is asking to be listened to even more closely. And so, with Haitink's head staying cocked, and Schiff offering us the first few tranquil bars, J 39 remembered what she hadn't finished saying about pullovers.

I leaned across and poked the German. Or the Austrian. Don't think I've got anything against foreigners, by the way. Admittedly, if he'd been a vast, beef-fed Englishman in a

World Cup T-shirt, I might have thought twice. In fact, in the case of the Austro-German, I did think twice. Like this. My first thought was: you're coming to hear music in my country, don't behave as if you are still in yours. And my second thought was: given where you come from, it's even worse to behave like this during Mozart. So I poked him with a joined tripod of thumb and first two fingers. Hard. J 38 turned instinctively, and I glared at him with a finger tapping my lips. J 39 stopped chattering, if only because her audience had been distracted. K 37 – me – went back to the music. Not that I could entirely concentrate on it. I felt jubilation rising in me like a sneeze. At last I'd done it, after all these years of provocation.

Later, of course, it became more complicated. During the final allegro, I caught myself wondering if the chap I poked had assumed it was OK to behave so expansively because everyone around him seemed to be doing the same, and it was his attempt to appear mannerly, rather than unmannerly: wenn in London . . . . Later, at home, Andrew applied all his usual logic in an attempt to deflate me. Putting down his whisky for a moment, he pleaded fake ignorance but wasn't it the case that old music like Bach and Handel and Mozart had been composed for royal or ducal courts, and wouldn't such patrons and their retinue have been strolling around, having dinner, picking their noses, throwing chicken bones at the harpist, flirting with their neighbours' wives and whatever while listening to their employee's tunes? But they weren't composed with that in mind, I said. How do you know, Andrew replied, surely those composers were aware of how their music would be listened to and either wrote music which they hoped would cover the background noise and chicken-bone-throwing, or, more likely, tried to write music which commanded such attention that the audience fell silent? And that – you see how Andrew argues – were it not for the challenging conditions under which their music was to be performed, the composers might have been satisfied with stuff of lower quality, attractiveness, or whatever it might be that makes an upcountry baronet briefly stop pizzicatoing his neighbour's wife's forearm? Did not all art thrive on difficulty and obstruction? Furthermore, this harmless neighbour of mine with his wing collar was probably a linear descendant of that upcountry baronet, simply behaving in the same way: he'd paid his money, and was entitled to listen as much or as little as he chose.

"In Vienna", I said, "when you went to the opera, twenty or thirty years ago, if you uttered the slightest cough, a flunky in knee-breeches and powdered wig would come over to you and give you a cough sweet."

"That must have put everyone off even more. You could always try it, though."

Andrew says he doesn't understand why I still go to concerts. I only complain, I only get enraged. I have a perfectly good sound system at home, a large collection of CDs, and tolerant neighbours. Why bother? I bother, I tell him, because if you are in a concert hall, and have paid money and taken time to go there, you listen to the music more carefully. Not from what you tell me, he replies: you seem to be distracted most of the time. Well, I would pay more attention if I wasn't distracted, I replied. And what would you pay more attention to, just as a purely theoretical question (you see how provoking Andrew can be?). I thought about this for a moment, and then said, The loud bits and the soft bits, to put it crudely. The loud bits, because however big and good your system, nothing can compare with the reality of a hundred or more musicians going at it full tilt in front of you, filling the air. And the soft bits, which is more paradoxical, because you'd think any sound system could reproduce that. But it can't. For instance, those opening bars of the larghetto floating across twenty yards of space, or fifty, or a hundred; though floating isn't the right word, because it implies time spent travelling, whereas though you can see the music on its way to you the sense of time is abolished, as is space, for that matter.

"So how was the Shostakovich?" Andrew asked. "Loud enough to drown the bastards out?" "Well," I said, "That's an interesting point. You know how it starts off with those huge climaxes? It made me realize what I mean about the loud bits. Everyone's making as much noise as possible, brass, timps, big bad drum, and you know what comes out over the top, cuts through it all? The xylophone. There was this woman bashing away and it came through clear as a bell. Now, if you'd heard that on a record you'd think it was the result of some fancy bit of engineering. Spotlighting, or whatever they call it. But here you knew that was how it was meant to sound, that he knew just what he was up to when he wrote it."

"So you had a good time?" "But it also made me realize it's the pitch that counts. The piccolo does the same. It's not just the cough or the sneeze and its volume, but how it cuts through the musical texture it's competing with. So you can't even relax in the loudest bits, is what that means."

"Cough sweets", said Andrew. "Otherwise, you know, I do think you'll go seriously, woof-ingly mad."

"Coming from you", I replied.

He knew what I meant. Let me tell you about Andrew. We've lived together for twenty or more years, since university. He works in the furniture department of the V & A. Every day, rain or shine, he cycles there from Islington. One side of London to the other, and back. On his journey he does two things: listens to opera on his Walkman, and looks out for firewood. I know, it doesn't sound likely, but he says you only have to look and you'll find things. Most days of the week he manages to fill his basket, enough for our evening fire, even though strictly speaking you shouldn't burn wood in a conservation area. So he goes from this one very civilized place to another, singing along to Bellini or whoever, while keeping an eye out for skips and fallen trees.

But that's not all. He crosses London twice a day in the middle of the rush hour, and even though he knows a lot of cut-throughs where the firewood hangs out, the traffic is usually terrible. And most car-drivers look out for other car-drivers. Buses, taxis, lorries; maybe motor-cyclists. But pedal cyclists are low on their list. And this makes Andrew hopping mad. There they are, sitting on their arses, pouring out fumes, one person to a car, unhealthy, environmentally abusive solipsists, and then they'll try and swerve into a two-yard gap to gain an advantage of six inches on another car without bothering to check for cyclists. Andrew shouts at them. Andrew, in mid-aria, Andrew, my civilized friend, companion and now ex-lover, Andrew, who has spent half the day poring over some exquisite piece of marquetry with a restorer, shouts, "You fucking cunt!" He also shouts, "I hope you get cancer!" He also shouts, "Drive under a fucking lorry!" "What about women drivers?" I ask.

"Oh, I don't call them cunts", he replies, brushing a crumb from his thigh. "'You fucking bitch!' That's what I shout at them."

Then off he pedals, looking for firewood and singing along to Teresa Berganza. These days he only does the abusive shouting. He used to bang on car roofs if a driver cut him up. Bang bang bang with a sheepskin-lined glove. It must sound like a thunder-machine from Strauss or Henze. He also used to snap their wing-mirrors back on their hinges, folding them in against the body of the car. That really irritates motorists. But he's stopped doing this; he had a scare about a year ago. This fellow caught up with him and tipped him off his bike and made various threatening suggestions. So Andrew stopped playing the thunder-machine and snapping wing-mirrors. Now he just calls them fucking cunts at the top of his voice. They can't object to that, because that's what they are, and they know it.

I started taking cough sweets to concerts. I would hand them out on the spot to offenders within my immediate reach, and to distant hackers during the interval. It wasn't a great success. For a start, I obviously couldn't leave them in their crankly wrappers; and most people would think twice before popping into their mouths an unwrapped sweet given them by a stranger. And the second problem was that I clearly didn't cut the same authority as an usher in knee-breeches and powdered wig. Some of those I accosted thought it was a friendly gesture on my part. Well, I certainly wasn't asking to be thanked.

It's hard to get it right, isn't it? Like when the performers themselves try to exert their will over noisy halls. I've seen Brendel turn away from the keyboard in the middle of a Beethoven sonata and briefly glare at some bronchitic bastard. But a) how does the pianist know exactly where to glare; b) how does the pianist know that the said bastard will even be aware that he is being rebuked; and c) since most of the loyal, quiet, throat-suppressing sympathizers in the audience will have noticed the performer's gesture, this in turn will distract them, and then they'll be worrying about whether the pianist's been distracted, and so on.

I decided that I needed authority, precision targeting, plus a change of technique. The unwrapped cough sweet was like an ambiguous gesture from cyclist to motorist: oh good, he approves of me swerving from lane to lane. None of that. I was going to bang on their roofs. But I am of reasonably sturdy physique. To the more effete and pigeon-chested concert-goer, I might look as if I had fallen off the front of a lorry.

To begin with, I moved from the stalls to the annex. That's the section which runs along the side of the auditorium, so that you sit facing out across the stalls. You can follow the conductor and police the audience with just a slow pan of the head; you can cover the front half of the terrace as well as the stalls. Secondly, I changed my clothes. Dark blue suit of a rather thick, sergey material; dark blue undecorated tie, and in the lapel a badge with a heraldic shield. I pitched the effect deliberately. An offender might very well mistake me for one of the Hall's official ushers; while my muscular condition suggested that I was quite capable of throwing him out if necessary. And thirdly, there was my change of technique. This usher would not discreetly hand out cough sweets. This usher would wait until the interval, and either accost them as they rose from their seats or follow them – the more ostentatiously the better – out into the bar or one of those undifferentiated areas with wide-screen views of the Thames.

"Excuse me, sir, but are you aware of the decibel level of the unmuffled cough?" They would look at me rather nervously, as I would make sure that my voice was also unmuffled. "It's reckoned at about 85", I would continue. "A fortissimo note on the trumpet is about the same." I quickly learnt not to give them the chance to explain how they'd picked up that nasty throat, how they'd never do it again, or whatever. "So, thank you, sir, we would be grateful . . . ." And I moved on, the lingering we endorsing my quasi-official presence.

With women I was different. There is, as Andrew had pointed out, a difference – a necessary difference – between You fucking cunt and You fucking bitch. And there was often the question of the male companion or husband who might feel within himself stirrings from the time when caves were daubed with ruddy bison in stylish freehand. "We do sympathize about the cough, Madam", I would say, in a lowered, almost medical voice. "But the orchestra and conductor find it quite unhelpful." This was, if anything, even more offensive, but they didn't realize it at the time: it was more the snapped-back mirror than the thundered roof.

But I did also want to bang on the roof. I wanted to be offensive. It seemed right. So I developed various lines of abuse. For instance, I would identify the offender, follow him (statistically it tended to be a him) to where he was standing with his interval coffee or half of lager, and ask, in what therapists would call a non-confrontational manner, "Excuse me, but do you like art? Do you go to museums and galleries?" This generally produced a positive answer, even if one tinged with suspicion, as if I might be about to produce a clipboard and run through a questionnaire. So I would quickly follow up my initial question. "And what would you say is your favourite painting? One of them, anyway?" People liked being asked this, and I might be rewarded with The Hay Wain or The Rokeby Venus or Monet's Water-lilies or whatever.

"Well, imagine this", I'd say with a polite cheerfulness. "You're standing in front of The Rokeby Venus, and I'm standing next to you, and while you're looking at it, at this incredibly famous picture which you love more than anything else in the world, I start gobbing at it, so that bits of the canvas are all covered with spit. I don't just do it once, but several times. What would you think about that?" I am still in my reasonable-man-not-quite-with-clipboard mode.

The answers vary between the poles of action and reflection, between "I'd call the guards" and "I'd think you were a nutter."

"Exactly," I reply, moving a little closer. "So don't" – and here I sometimes give them a poke in the shoulder or on the chest, a poke which was a little harder than they expected, "don't cough in the middle of Mozart. It's like gobbing on The Rokeby Venus."

Some of them look sheepish, some as if they've been caught child-molesting. Some say, "Who do you think you are?" And I say, "Just someone who's paid for his seat like you." Note that I never claim to be an official. Then I add: "And I'll be keeping my eye on you."

Some of them lie. "It's hay fever", they say, and I answer, "Bring the hay in with you, did you?" One student type was apologetic about his timing: "I thought I knew the piece. I thought there was a crescendo coming up, not a diminuendo." I gave him the full glare, as you might imagine.

But I can't pretend everyone is either accommodating, or crestfallen. Pin-striped chaps, bolshie buggers, macho types with tittling women in tow: they can get tricky. I might run through one of my routines and they'd say, "Who precisely do you think you are?" or, "Oh, just bugger off, will you?" – things like that, not really addressing the issue, and some will give me a look as if I'm the weirdo and turn their backs. I don't like that sort of behaviour, I think it's discourteous, so I might give the arm that's holding the drink a little nudge, and that helps turn them round towards me, and if they're by themselves I'll go up close and say, "Know what, you're a fucking cunt, and I'll be keeping my eye on you." They don't like being spoken to in this way, mostly. Of course, if there's a woman with them I moderate my language. "What's it like being a" (pause) "selfish bastard?" One of them summoned a Festival Hall usher. I could see his plan, so I went and sat down with a modest glass of water, slipped off my heraldic lapel-badge and became horribly reasonable. "Ah, I'm glad he's brought you over. I wanted to ask if you have a policy with persistent and unmuffled coughers. I mean, presumably at some point you take steps to exclude them. Could you explain the complaints procedure, because I'm sure many people in the audience tonight would be happy to join me in asking you to refuse future bookings from this, er, gentleman."

Andrew keeps thinking up practical solutions. Not that they're any help. He says I should go to the Wigmore Hall instead. He says I should stay at home and listen to my records. He says I spend so much time being a vigilante that I can't possibly be concentrating on the music. I say I don't want to go to the Wigmore Hall. I'm saving chamber music for later. I want to go to the Festival Hall, the Albert Hall and the Barbican, and no one's going to stop me. Andrew says I should sit in the cheap seats, in the choir or among the Prommers. He says people who sit in expensive seats are like people who drive BMWs, Range Rovers and big Volvos, just fucking cunts, what do I expect?

I tell him I have two proposals for concert hall boards. The first would involve the installation of seat spotlights – like the overhead lights in aeroplanes – and if someone made a noise above a certain agreed level – one specified in the programme, but also printed on the ticket so that non-programme-buyers wouldn't be discriminated against – then the light over their seat would come on and the person would have to sit there as if in the stocks for the rest of the concert. My second suggestion would be more discreet. Every seat in the hall would be wired, and a small electric shock administered, whose force would vary according to the strength of the occupant's cough, sniffle or sneeze. This would – as laboratory experiments on various species have shown – tend to discourage the offender from offending again.

Andrew said that apart from legal considerations, he foresaw two objections to my plan. The first was that if you gave a human being an electric shock, he or she might very well respond by making more noise than he or she had done in the first place, which would be somewhat counterproductive. And secondly, much as he wanted to encourage my notion, he thought the practical effect of electrocuting concert-goers might well be that people would be less rather than more willing to book tickets. Though he supposed that if the London Philharmonic played to a completely empty hall, then there wouldn't be any coughs or sneezes or digital-watch alarms at all. So yes, that would achieve my aim, though without bums on seats, the orchestra might need a considerably higher level of sponsorship. Except, of course, that the sponsors themselves wouldn't be able to come to their own concerts.

Andrew can be so provoking, don't you think? I asked him if he had ever tried listening to the still, sad music of humanity while someone was using a mobile phone.

"I wonder what instrument that would be played on", he replied. "Perhaps not an instrument at all. What you would do is strap a thousand or so people into concert hall seats and quietly pass an electric current through them while telling them not to make a noise or they'll get a bigger shock. You'd get muted groans and moans and assorted muffled squeaks – and that's the still, sad music of humanity."

"You're such a cynic", I replied. "Actually, I don't think it's such a bad plan."

Last week I pushed someone down the stairs. He had been especially offensive: holding hands, cuddling, chattering, programme-rustling, plus excessive turnings of the head and looking around. He'd conspicuously failed to respond to my rebukes as well. Positively rude. So I caught him on the ankle going down those side-stairs from level 2A. He went down on his face, and there was a fair amount of blood. He was a heavy man. The woman he was with, who hadn't been any more civil to me, began screaming. I thought, as I turned away, that'll teach you to treat Sibelius's violin concerto with more respect.

It's about respect, isn't it? And if you weren't taught it young, you have to be taught it later. The true test, the only test, is whether we're slowly getting more civilized, or whether we aren't. Don't you agree?

September 4, 1998

The Red-Haired Girl

By Penelope Fitzgerald

Hackett, Holland, Parsons, Charrington and Dubois all studied in Paris, in the atelier of Vincent Bonvin. Dubois, although his name sounded French, wasn't, and didn't speak any either. None of them did except Hackett.

In the summer of 1882 they made up a party to go to Brittany. That was because they admired Bastien-Lepage, which old Bonvin certainly didn't, and because they wanted somewhere cheap, somewhere with characteristic types, absolutely natural, busy with picturesque occupations, and above all, *plein air*. "Your work cannot be really good unless you have caught a cold doing it", said Hackett.

They were poor enough, but they took a certain quantity of luggage – only the necessities. Their canvases needed rigging like small craft putting out of harbour, and the artists themselves, for *plein air* work, had brought overcoats, knickerbockers, gaiters, boots, wideawakes, broad straw hats for sunny days. They tried, to begin with, St Briac-sur-Mer, which had been recommended to them in Paris, but it didn't suit. On, then, to Palourde, on the coast near Cancale. All resented the time spent moving about. It wasn't in the spirit of the thing, they were artists, not sightseers.

At Palourde, although it looked, and was, larger than St Briac, there was, if anything, less room. The Palourdais had never come across artists before, considered them as rich rather than poor, and wondered why they did not go to St Malo. Holland, Parsons, Charrington and Dubois, however, each found a room of sorts. What about their possessions? There were sail-lofts and potato-cellars in Palourde, but, it seemed, not an inch of room to spare. Their clothes, books and painting material had to go in some boats pulled up above the foreshore, awaiting repairs. They were covered with a piece of tarred sailcloth and roped down. Half the morning would have to be spent getting out what was wanted. Hackett, as interpreter, was obliged to ask whether there was any risk of their being stolen. The reply was that no one in Palourde wanted such things.

It was agreed that Hackett should take what appeared to be the only room in the constricted Hotel du Port. "Right under the rafters", he wrote to his Intended, "a bed, a chair, a basin, a broc of cold water brought up once a day, no view from the window, but I shan't of course paint in my room anyway. I have propped up the canvases I brought with me against the wall. That gives me the sensation of having done something. The food, so far, you wouldn't approve of. Black porridge, later on pieces of black porridge left over from the morning and fried, fish soup with onions, onion soup with fish. The thing is to understand these people well, try to share their devotion to onions, and above all to secure a good model" – he decided not to add "who must be a young girl, otherwise I haven't much chance of any of the London exhibitions."

The Hotel du Port was inconveniently placed at the top of the village. It had no restaurant, but Hackett was told that he could be served, if he wanted it, at half-past six o'clock. The ground floor was taken up with the bar, so this service would be in a very small room at the back, opening off the kitchen.

After Hackett had sat for some time at a narrow table covered with rose-patterned oilcloth, the door opened sufficiently for a second person to edge into the room. It was a red-haired girl, built for hard use and hard wear, who without speaking put down a bowl of fish soup. She and the soup between them filled the room with a sharp, cloudy odour, not quite disagreeable, but it wasn't possible for her to get in and out, concentrating always on not spilling anything, without knocking the back of the chair and the door itself, first with her elbows, then with her rump. The spoons and the saltbox on the table trembled as though in a railway carriage. Then the same manoeuvre again, this time bringing a loaf of dark bread and a carafe of cider. No more need to worry after that, there was no more to come.

"I think I've found rather a jolly-looking model already", Hackett told the others. They, too, had not done so badly. They had set up their easels on the quay, been asked, as far as they could make out, to move them further away from the moorings, done so "with a friendly smile", said Charrington – "we find that goes a long way." They hadn't risked asking anyone to model for them, just started some sea-pieces between the handfuls of wind and rain. "We might come up to the hotel tonight and dine with you. There's nothing but fish soup in our digs."

Hackett discouraged them.

The hotelier's wife, when he had made the right preliminary enquiries from her about the red-haired girl, had answered – as she did, however, on all subjects – largely with silences. He didn't learn who her parents were, or even her family name. Her given name was Annik. She worked an all-day job at the Hotel du Port, but she had one and a half hours free after her lunch and if she wanted to spend that being drawn or painted, well, there were no objections. Not in the hotel, however, where, as he could see, there was no room.

"I paint *en plein air*", said Hackett.

"You'll find plenty of that."

"I shall pay her, of course."

"You must make your own arrangements."

He spoke to the girl at dinner, during the few moments when she was conveniently trapped. When she had quite skilfully allowed the door to shut behind her and, soup-dish in hand, was recovering her balance, he said:

"Anny, I want to ask you something."

"I'm called Annik", she said. It was the first time he had heard her speak.

"All the girls are called that. I shall call you Anny. I've spoken about you to the patronne."

"Yes, she told me."

Anny was a heavy breather, and the whole tiny room seemed to expand and deflate as she stood pondering.

"I shall want you to come to the back door of the hotel, I mean the back steps down to the rue de Dol. Let us say tomorrow, at twelve forty-five."

"I don't know about the forty-five", she said. "I can't be sure about that."

"How do you usually know the time?" She was silent. He thought it was probably a matter of pride and she did not want to agree to anything too easily. But possibly she couldn't tell the time. She might be stupid to the degree of idiocy.

The Hotel du Port had no courtyard. Like every other house in the street, it had a flight of stone steps to adapt to the change of level. After lunch the shops shut for an hour and the women of Palourde sat or stood, according to their age, on the top step and knitted or did crochet. They didn't wear costume any more, they wore white linen caps and jackets, long skirts, and, if they weren't going far, carpet slippers.

Anny was punctual to the minute. "I shall want you to stand quite still on the top step, with your back to the door. I've asked them not to open it."

Anny, also, was wearing carpet slippers. "I can't just stand here doing nothing."

He allowed her to fetch her crochet. Give a little, take a little. He was relieved, possibly a bit disappointed, to find how little interest they caused in the rue de Dol. He was used to being watched, quite openly, over his shoulder, as if he was giving a comic performance. Here even the children didn't stop to look.

"They don't care about our picture", he said, trying to amuse her. He would have liked a somewhat gentler expression. Certainly she was not a beauty. She hadn't the white skin of the dreamed-of red-haired girl, in fact her face and neck were covered with a faint but noticeable hairy down, as though proof against all weathers.

"How long will it take?" she asked.

"I don't know. As God disposes! An hour will do for today."

"And then you'll pay me?" "No", he said, "I shan't do that. I shall pay you when the whole thing's finished. I shall keep a record of the time you've worked, and if you like you can keep one as well."

As he was packing up his box of charcoals he added: "I shall want to make a few colour notes tomorrow, and I should like you to wear a red shawl." It seemed that she hadn't one. "But you could borrow one, my dear. You could borrow one, since I ask you particularly."

She looked at him as though he were an imbecile.

"You shouldn't have said 'Since I ask you particularly'", Parsons told him that evening. "That will have turned her head."

"It can't have done", said Hackett.

"Did you call her 'my dear'?"

"I don't know, I don't think so."

"I've noticed you say 'particularly' with a peculiar intonation, which may well have become a matter of habit", said Parsons, nodding sagely.

This is driving me crazy, thought Hackett. He began to feel a division which he had never so much as dreamed of in Paris between himself and his fellow students. They had been working all day, having managed to rent a disused and indeed almost unusable shed on the quay. It had once been part of the market where the fishermen's wives did the triage, sorting out the catch by size. Hackett, as before, had done the interpreting. He had plenty of time, since Anny could only be spared for such short intervals. But at least he had been true to his principles. Holland, Parsons, Charrington and Dubois weren't working in the open air at all. Difficulties about models forgotten, they were sketching each other in the shed. The background of Palourde's not very picturesque jetty could be dashed in later.

Anny appeared promptly for the next three days to stand, with her crochet, on the back steps. Hackett didn't mind her blank expression, having accepted from the first that she was never likely to smile. The red shawl, though – that hadn't appeared. He could, perhaps, buy one in St Malo. He ached for the contrast between the copper-coloured hair and the scarlet shawl. But he felt it wrong to introduce something from outside Palourde.

"Anny, I have to tell you that you've disappointed me."

"I told you I had no red shawl."

"You could have borrowed one."

Charrington, who was supposed to understand women, and even to have had a great quarrel with Parsons about some woman or other, only said: "She can't borrow what isn't there. I've been trying ever since we came here to borrow a decent tin-opener. I've tried to make it clear that I'd give it back."

Best to leave the subject alone. But the moment Anny turned up next day he found himself saying: "You could borrow one from a friend, that was what I meant."

"I haven't any friends", said Anny. Hackett paused in the business of lighting his pipe. "An empty life for you, then, Anny."

"You don't know what I want", she said, very low.

"Oh, everybody wants the same things. The only difference is what they will do to get them."

"You don't know what I want, and you don't know what I feel", she said, still in the same mutter. There was, however, a faint note of something more than the contradiction that came so naturally to her, and Hackett was a good-natured man.

"I'm sorry I said you disappointed me, Anny. The truth is I find it rather a taxing business, standing here drawing in the street."

"I don't know why you came here in the first place. There's nothing here, nothing at all. If it's oysters you want, they're better at Cancale. There's nothing here to tell one morning from another, except to see if it's raining . . . . Once they brought in three drowned bodies, two men and a boy, a whole boat's crew, and laid them out on the tables in the fish market, and you could see blood and water running out of their mouths . . . . You can spend your whole life here, wash, pray, do your work, and all the time you might just as well not have been born."

She was still speaking so that she could scarcely be heard. The passers-by went unnoticing down Palourde's badly paved Street. Hackett felt disturbed. It had never occurred to him that she would speak, without prompting, at such length.

"I've received a telegram from Paris", said Parsons, who was standing at the shed door. "It's taken its time about getting here. They gave it me at the post office."

"What does it say?" asked Hackett, feeling it was likely to be about money.

"Well, that he's coming – Bonvin, I mean. As is my custom every summer, I am touring the coasts – it's a kind of informal inspection, you see. Expect me, then, on the 27th for dinner at the Hotel du Port."

"It's impossible." Parsons suggested that, since Dubois had brought his banjo with him, they might get up some kind of impromptu entertainment. But he had to agree that one couldn't associate old Bonvin with entertainment.

He couldn't, surely, be expected from Paris before six. But when they arrived, all of them except Hackett carrying their portfolios, at the hotel's front door, they recognized, from the moment it opened, the voice of Bonvin. Hackett looked round, and felt his head swim. The bar, dark, faded, pickled in its own long-standing odours, crowded with stools and barrels, with the air of being older than Palourde, as though Palourde had been built round it without daring to disturb it, was swept and emptied now except for a central table and chairs such as Hackett had never seen in the hotel. At the head of the table sat old Bonvin. "Sit down, gentlemen! I am your host!" The everyday malicious dry voice, but a different Bonvin, in splendid seaside dress, a yellow waistcoat, a cravat. Palourde was indifferent to artists, but Bonvin had imposed himself as a professor.

"They are used to me here. They keep a room for me which I think is not available to other guests and they are always ready to take a little trouble for me when I come."

The artists sat meekly down, while the patronne herself served them with a small glass of greenish-white muscadet.

"I am your host", repeated Bonvin. "I can only say that I am delighted to see pupils, for the first time, in Palourde, but I assure you I have others as far away as Corsica. Once a teacher, always a teacher! I sometimes think it is a passion which outlasts even art itself."

They had all assured each other, in Paris, that old Bonvin was incapable of teaching anything. Time spent in his atelier was squandered. But here, in the strangely transformed bar of the Hotel du Port, with a quite inadequate drink in front of them, they felt overtaken by destiny. The patronne shut and locked the front door to keep out the world who might disturb the professor. Bonvin, not, after all, looking so old, called upon them to show their portfolios.

Hackett had to excuse himself to go up to his room and fetch the four drawings which he had made so far. He felt it an injustice that he had to show his things last.

Bonvin asked him to hold them up one by one, then to lay them out on the table. To Hackett he spoke magniloquently, in French.

"Yes, they are bad", he said, "but, M Hackett, they are bad for two distinct reasons. In the first place, you should not draw the view from the top of a street if you cannot manage the perspective, which even a child, following simple mechanical rules, can do. The relationship in scale of the main figure to those lower down is quite, quite wrong. But there is something else amiss.

"You are an admirer, I know, of Bastien-Lepage, who has

said, 'There is nothing really lasting, nothing that will endure, except the sincere expression of the actual conditions of life.' Conditions in the potato patch, in the hayfield, at the washtub, in the open street! That is pernicious nonsense. Look at this girl of yours. Evidently she is not a professional model, for she doesn't know how to hold herself. I see you have made a note that the colour of the hair is red, but that is the only thing I know about her. She's standing against the door like a beast waiting to be put back in its stall. It's your intention, I am sure, to do the finished version in the same way, in the dust of the street. Well, your picture will say nothing and it will be nothing. It is only in the studio that you can bring out the heart of the subject, and that is what we are sent into this world to do, M Hackett, to paint the experiences of the heart."

(– Gibbering dotard, you can talk till your teeth fall out. I shall go on precisely as I have been doing, even if I can only paint her for an hour and a quarter a day. –) An evening of nameless embarrassment, with Hackett's friends coughing, shuffling, eating noisily, asking questions to which they knew the answer, and telling anecdotes of which they forgot the endings. Anny had not appeared, evidently she was considered unworthy, the patronne came in again, bringing not soup but the very height of Brittany's grand-occasion cuisine, a fricassee of chicken. Who would have thought there were chickens in Palourde?

Hackett woke in what he supposed were the small hours. So far he had slept dreamlessly in Palourde, had never so much as lighted his bedside candle. Probably, he thought, Bonvin made the same unpleasant speech wherever he went. The old impostor was drunk with power – not with anything else, only half a bottle of muscadet and, later, a bottle of gros-plant between the six of them. The sky had begun to thin and pale. It came to him that what had been keeping him awake was not an injustice of Bonvin's, but of his own. What had been the experiences of Anny's heart? – Bonvin, with his dressing cases and book-boxes, left early. The horse omnibus stopped once a week in the little Place François-René de Chateaubriand, at the entrance to the village. Having made his formal farewells, Bonvin caught the omnibus. Hackett was left in good time for his appointment with Anny.

She did not come that day, nor the next day, nor the day after. On the first evening he was served by the bootboy, pitifully worried about getting in and out of the door, on the second by the hotel laundrywoman, on the third by the patronne. "Where is Anny?" She did not answer. For that in itself Hackett was prepared, but he tried again. "Is she ill?" "No, not ill". "Has she taken another job?" "No." He was beginning, he realized, in the matter of this plain and sullen girl, to sound like an anxious lover. "Shall I see her again?" He got no answer.

– Had she drowned herself? The question reared up in his mind, like a savage dog getting up from its sleep. She had hardly seemed to engage herself enough with life, hardly seemed to take enough interest in it to wish no more of it. Boredom, though, and the withering sense of insignificance can bring one as low as grief. He had felt the breath of it at his ear when Bonvin had told him – for that was what it came to – that there was no hope of his becoming an artist. Anny was stupid, but no one is too stupid to despair.

There was no police station in Palourde, and if Anny were truly drowned, they would say nothing about it at the Hotel du Port. Hackett had been in enough small hotels to know that they did not discuss anything that was bad for business. The red-haired body might drift anywhere, might be washed ashore anywhere between Pointe du Grouin and Cap Prehel.

That night it was the laundrywoman's turn to dish up the fish soup. Hackett thought of confiding in her, but did not need to. She said to him: "You mustn't keep asking the patronne about Anny, it disturbs her." Anny, it turned out, had been dismissed for stealing from the hotel – some money, and a watch. "You had better have a look through your things", the laundrywoman said, "and see there's nothing missing. One often doesn't notice till a good while afterwards."

September 11, 1998

Bookcruncher

By Tibor Fischer

He pushed open the door marked STAFF ONLY. He took a look at the noticeboard to see if there was anything new. There wasn't.

A number of shoplifter alerts were posted with crude characteristics: smelly, Irish, steals Atlases. Or: horn-rim glasses, long overcoat, sandwiches, fond of gardening. Some sales and turnover stats. Vacancies at other branches. He opened the cupboard where he knew the coffee would be and got the kettle to boil. Into the jar that served as receptacle for coffee money, he counted out the change, two dimes and a nickel.

Not caring about coffee was a feat he congratulated himself on. What the reputable brands were, he had no idea. He didn't waste a second fussing over coffee, how many spoonfuls, how much water, how much milk, how much sugar. Coffee was something many people could get worked up about. He had one over them.

He shot through some new books, and then tried a few phone calls. But no one was there.

So he sipped his coffee and enjoyed the comfy chair.

He felt okay, he told himself. Truthfully, no, not okay . . . more than okay . . . he felt good. At ease. He spent fifteen minutes thinking how unimportant birthdays were. Then several minutes considering whether he might be wrong. Followed by half an hour pondering that sitting on your own in a bookshop office on your birthday with a couple of bananas and half a loaf of half-dry bread for supper, although he felt fine about it, might seem wretched to others, and was he worried about looking miserable? Did what other people thought matter?

Eventually he got tired of thinking about it.

There was a pleasant atmosphere to the room. Snug. It was a pity he didn't work here, but anyway, he had to get to work.

The next morning he emerged unobserved from Natural History and walked out and made his way towards the Port Authority.

As he was crossing a quiet street, a skinny black man approached him.

"I've got something for you." He made no response and strode on in that unlistening way that forms big cities, sensing his failure to look poor, crazy and dangerous enough to repel contact. The poor and crazy he was pretty good at but he was just not getting anywhere near dangerous. But he stopped when the black man offered him an elephant.

He looked into the trailer, and, irrefutably, it was an Indian elephant. A young elephant, young enough to fit into the horse-trailer, old enough to look disgruntled and tired of the elephant game. Shaking his head he carried on.

"You need this elephant", exhorted the salesman, transmitting such urgency that for a moment, he experienced the conviction that what he did indeed need was an elephant, this elephant. This emotion vanished as quickly as it had come. That was what it was all about essentially: people telling you you needed things, or that you enjoyed things, and then discovering that you didn't.

"A hundred dollars. A hundred dollars is all I'm asking." A bargain. Too good to pass up. But he didn't need an elephant, a dodgy one to boot, that much he had learned in his thirty-three years. He tended to be defined in the negative; he was someone who didn't need an elephant.

Although more desperate, the salesman was almost by definition a more interesting person since he needed to sell an elephant. Above all, he didn't have a place to put the elephant, since he didn't have a place to put himself. But perhaps that was the greatest gift, the knack of allowing yourself to be convinced and staying that way.

He went to his locker, and rummaged round. He liberated the Bookcruncher T-shirt from the grip of other apparel and changed.

He didn't like the T-shirt any more, he found it embarrassing. Bookcruncher in a bold arc at the top, the first two lines of the *Iliad* in the middle and underneath, in lower case, Fear Me. It was the kind of item you had made when you were young and belligerent. A woman who had started lecturing him on dress sense in a diner, despite his flagrantly reading two books to deflect her, had been horrified to discover, when, under interrogation, he had calculated that the T-shirt was twelve years old. Genuinely horrified. But he didn't throw it away, since he never threw anything away, and like most unwanted items of clothing it was indestructible.

Now he had the option of going round the corner to the Paramount Hotel for a quick wash, or going to Sylvana's for a more comprehensive job; he was on for a shower, but the deal with Sylvana was doing the washing-up and dusting in exchange for towellage. Sylvana had a lot of books which were phenomenally difficult to dust and since he had now read all of them he found it hard to get involved.

He strolled over to the Paramount and entered the Gents where he stripped to the waist, freshened up, flossed lengthily and realized he didn't feel very industrious. He went there regularly and had never been bothered. Unintentionally, he supposed, he managed poor and crazy as done by the rich and foreign.

Afterwards it was the Cuban restaurant and the special. He always ordered the special; this relieved him of the duty of studying the menu, and the staff of the duty of trying to unload the special. He was up to 1884, and he reached for his copy of *The Remarkable History of Sir Thomas Bart* which was remarkable only in being boring, and *The Story of Charles Strange*, which wasn't strange but boring.

The garlic chicken and rice with black beans came after

only three pages. As he made the first incision he wondered whether his father was dead.

They said you only became a full man once your father died. One afternoon would he suddenly feel a surge of power out of the blue and know? That would be the only way he'd get any news about his father.

He wondered how often he had that thought. Once every day for ten years? Twice every day? Three times every two days? How much time was that he had wasted? For five minutes a go? Ten minutes? You wasted so much time with the same thoughts. People complained about having to do the same things, about having to eat the same things, about having to wear the same clothes, but they never had any problem thinking the same thoughts. He realized this was another thought almost as frequent as the preceding one.

In the booth opposite him, a man in a porkpie hat, reading a newspaper, complained about the special.

That was the one thing he could thank his father for: he could and would eat anything without a murmur. It was not so much that his father had been a bad cook, but when his mother had left, the food had always been tasteless and stunningly unvarying: sausages, black pudding, and pork chops. Other carnal effects in danger of going off in his father's shop had been thrown in very occasionally. He wondered how often he thought that? Every time he saw someone fussing in a restaurant or leaving their food. Mealtimes, he had learned a long time ago, were something to be crossed.

You were granted immunity to your own thoughts, he decided, it was close to impossible to bore yourself. If you had to sit next to someone who would regularly say that's one thing I can thank my father for and mealtimes are something to be crossed you would be gibbering within two days. So maturity is: when you stop having new sermonlets and you just drive ceaselessly round the roundabouts you've already built.

Nevertheless he relished the rice pudding, bruised with a

little cinnamon and the coffee: it was good to go wild periodically. He mostly avoided the final thought of the paternal package – what was sad was not that they hated each other, but simply that there was nothing there. He had sonned adequately and he wished his father could have pretended a little. After some years he had been granted a partial understanding of his father, when on a train, he had seen one of his friends from school. He had not talked to him for five years, but he had not gone over to talk to him: he had nothing to say. It was funny, was it not, in a world where a satellite could tell your brand of toothpaste, where you could blast a million words 10,000 miles away in the lowering of a finger, where you could wallow in sitcom from any continent, where there was no hiding and no silence, he didn't know where his father was and he had nothing to say to him?

"You read a lot", said the behatted kvetch indicating the two novels he had open. He nodded, because there was no denying it and because he didn't want to put up the ante for a conversation.

"Books aren't life."

"No, they're better", he replied, and flipped through the thirty-two library cards in his wallet to remove his one credit card to pay.

This was twenty-first-century vagrancy. An ocean away, in the rain small sums of money carrying his name made the pilgrimage to a bank in Cambridge; meanwhile in London, small American debts trudged to an address where a cheque would be signed in an acceptable approximation of his signature by Elsa, giving him the right to plastic.

He felt good. Rice pudding and coffee goodness. And a no-one-else-in-the-restaurant-doing-what-he-did goodness. No one else in New York. Probably no one else in the world.

On his way to the Public Library, he stopped off at the Post Office to see what had appeared. One cheque, three months late. A book to review; that would be 300 words saying what it was like, and 300 words saying what it wasn't like: fine. An invitation to a conference.

Several letters from Elsa – a birthday batch of correspondence. These days he always suffered from a temptation to put her letters straight into the bin, because over the last few years there had been nothing new. She had the same job, the same flat, and she employed the same expressions of concern and coaxing. He would have thought she would have got as tired of writing these sugardrops as he was of reading them but no: they were her roundabouts.

But then Elsa was tenacious and that was only one of her virtues. Crunchy, you can't expect me to make the first move, was a phrase that turned up every fifth letter and was, he surmised, totally unironic, despite Elsa having made every move from one to a thousand, and having used every weapon in the feminine arsenal from the smooth pebble to the shoulder-launched missile.

A wake of pink envelopes, cabinetloads of cards and other affection-heavy baubles had trailed him around the world: marzipan hippos, beanbag lions, furry diaries, a Bible keyring (surely the peak of incongruity since he had nowhere to live), chocolate breasts, tins of baked beans, inflatable lips, wind-up miniature Christmas trees, all bearing the message of softness. During periods of intense activity, she wrote almost every day; the bestial incarnations of the heart hunted him down: smiling bears, cheery dolphins came with the messages for someone special, thinking of you makes me happy. Along came the dejected rabbits, lugubrious moles and forlorn kittens with the tag, missing you. Elsa's supply of any object or animal capable of an alliance with endearment was apparently endless despite her being a university graduate, thirty-two, a woman of good taste and half of her communications failing to reach him.

No real reason why she had chosen him. He knew his chief merit was that he had no demerits. He wouldn't beat her, he wouldn't go chasing after other women, he wouldn't drink or blow their money at the bookie's, he wouldn't make her watch football on the television, or defecate on the floor. Like the legless tortoise in the joke, you would find him where you left him. He had been tempted by Elsa's repeated insistence that there was room aplenty in her flat, that he could do his work there. He wouldn't take up much space, and his upkeep was minimal. It wouldn't be a bad arrangement.

The only reason he didn't take it up was that he didn't want it; and he knew if he yielded it would remove the possibility of her finding a proper happiness. Was it nobility or just recognition that he would be nulling her life?

Every now and then silences of a few months' duration opened up, while Elsa's unsuccessful romances would be digested. A male silhouette would be spotted peripherally after Elsa went off on a holiday. A one-off reference to a forester met on a beach, a voice agent met on a cruise. Her liaisons seemed to be only as long as hotel beds.

It was good to see that Upstairs didn't just punish the freaks. While Elsa's looks would never stop traffic, she was intelligent, employed, considerate, a good cook, had a job in which she met people all the time, but she still spent nights prowling a double bed, although all she wanted to do was to hose a man down with tenderness.

He never understood those who thought being different was stimulating or valuable. Anyone who has been on the outside knows how cold it is.

He went over to the Public Library, found a quiet corner and loaded up. In the right *Three Weeks in Mopetown*, in the left *If I were God*. People often looked at him, but no one said anything.

The academic roundabout came, as it did nearly every day.

Why hadn't he got an academic job? Probably because he didn't want one. But he loved stepping out of the dark and shooting them in the back. Repeatedly. He loved the unfairness of it.

He would start off with by mentioning something obvious, so they hoped they had an audience worth showing off to.

Then he would usher in something rare, to show he was heavy, to get an eyebrow raised. Finally something truly obscure, only one or two copies in existence. To really scare them. It was easy. He did the nineteenth-century people by going back to the eighteenth; he did the eighteenth by using the seventeenth, the seventeenth clobbered by the sixteenth. It was easy, you only had to move a mere ten or fifteen years out of their fief to unsettle them. Then some would smile with relief, and say it was not their beat. How could you understand writers if you didn't know what came before, what they read? What the people they read had read? Those who took refuge in their era, he would go back and strafe again to show them that was no protection. That's why he did the reviews.

He put down *If I were God*. 1884 and counting. Getting the books in the right order was impossible and he couldn't be as neat as he'd like to be. He had to zig-zag.

The Idea had come to him thirteen years ago on the third floor of the University Library, reading a letter by the extremely dead Pope Pius II: "Without letters, every age is blind." And he wondered what you would see if you had all the letters, if you had read everything ever written? He was already living in the library by that point, which was perhaps the start.

Or had Paris been the start? He had backpacked there with Tom. Short of money, deeply uncool, they wandered around hoping to accrue chic and excitement. They had been amazed at the number of hotels in the quartier Latin and how full they all were. After two hours of walking around, they found one that had a free room, but they didn't have the money. They were offered a lesson in why people booked rooms at the height of the tourist season.

Three times they had walked past the bookshop; he had astonished himself with his self-control. The fourth time, he suggested to Tom they go in.

He had known about Shakespeare & Co and what it was. He had been young then, fairly ignorant, but alert enough to know about Joyce and Eliot being bandits. Once inside he was disabled by the choice, but Tom who had no time for books, went up to the counter to ask the crumpled man for hotel ideas. They had never been in Paris before let alone the book-shop, but the man had clearly seen them a thousand times.

He sighed: "If you're really stuck, you can stay here for one night. That's one night."

So he spent his first night in Paris in a bookshop, or more significantly he spent his first night in a bookshop in Paris. Tom went out to have a kebab, and then returned to talk to two American girls who were also in for the night and eating yoghurt, while Shakespeare & Co became his favourite book-shop. He didn't eat and he didn't sleep all night because he was so fascinated by the American editions he had never seen before.

He had watched the sun come up over Notre Dame and remembered how supposedly Faust had arrived in Paris, his baggage bulging with newly printed Gutenberg Bibles to sell, and how he had been encouraged to get lost by the Parisian manuscript guilds who didn't want their action cut into.

It had unstoppered him. You didn't have to leave when the bookshop closed. You stayed and carried on reading. He was already spending so much time in local bookshops that he was pegged as a shoplifter, but now he realized he could spend many more hours in bookshops. But he hadn't sensed it was the start. Just holiday fun.

The start had been in attendance that evening in the University Library, when he had been accidentally locked in. Then he had started staying in occasionally throughout the night because he didn't want to leave. He was never discov-ered; the staff came round at closing time, but it was easy to hide in the nocturnal stacks of a quiet top floor and then unconceal yourself in the morning.

True the phone call from his father had been part of the start. After his first term, he found himself cut off. His father had missed out on university; had at sixteen, as he often pub-licized, gone straight into butchering. The encouragement he had received to go to university, he discovered, had merely been encouragement to go. He found himself adrift with just enough change to fill a trouser pocket.

Hardly the greatest cruelty the world had seen. He could have found a job, but he decided to cut his expenses by giving up his room, putting most of his stuff into storage, staying in the library at night, reading most of the time, then walking over to the college in the morning where he would use one of the communal bathrooms; followed by some shopping, then a saunter back to the library.

He had none of the standard student expenses: he didn't go anywhere. From arriving at Cambridge till he left, he didn't leave, apart from once accompanying Elsa and some others in a countryside foray for pubs. He didn't go to the cinema or clubbing. Buying clothes was out. Eating properly was out. Buying books was out. Boozing was out. There was the grant, the scholarship and the hardship fund. He did some work in the University Library during the holidays, so everyone was used to seeing him around. And his life wasn't just the UL; he'd pop into the other libraries for some variety and a change of pace.

An uncomfortable awareness touched him that there was no one else who had his tastes: that he was a part of the apart. Elsa was constantly friendly to him, but they had little overlap. Nevertheless he had some fun. One afternoon he was picked up in Silver Street and conducted back to a bedsit by a woman who worked as a cleaner at the hospital. "Uncle Phil", she said, addressing him as he struggled to loosen her grip on his arm and to remember whether he had ever seen her before. "Fancy meeting you here, why not come back to my place?" Some great passion, he had imagined, was engulfing him; for a week he tended only amorous poetry, but of course Uncle Phil could be found on any street at any time. He learned a number of things: he cottoned on to why most people would do almost anything for sex, that her interest in him had nothing to do with him, and that everyone gets one free fuck.

When she had seized him he had almost shaken her off because he had books to read, but he was glad he had got that out of the way.

Then there was the party when just as he was regretting not staying in the library, he was so bored, two women stripped off. He felt like applauding, but hadn't. The bafflement of the males was interesting and it took him a few years to diagnose what was going on; the free parties were either intimidated by the audacity of undressing, or were unconcerned by women whose genitalia were common knowledge; but inevitably, there was Kev from Belfast who did both of them over the rickety ironing-board in the laundry-room. Kev was the only one apart from him who didn't complain about the college food. It was plain even then who was going to get on.

He picked at a bit of bean on his Bookcruncher T-shirt, which had fallen in and coalesced with the gable of Achilles's A.

But he had dedicated himself to reading everything.

Then, on reflection, he realized he couldn't do that. But everything in English. Everything in book form. He had read a good amount, he had been averaging three or four books a day since eleven. Although he had wasted some time in irrelevant topics. He knew more about Chinese history than was healthy for anyone but a Chinese historian for instance.

He had never explained his mission to anyone, because he didn't want anyone to know if he failed, and because he wasn't sure what the point was. He sensed there was an answer at the end, but he had no idea what it would be or what he would do with it. Perhaps he would write something original. After all how can you be sure you're writing something original if you haven't read everything before?

The numbers were daunting. A few hundred books to 1500. Some ten thousand to 1600. Eighty thousand to 1700. Three hundred thousand to 1800. Then things go crazy. Much of it was recloaking. Much of it was dross. Much of it was brief. But if he hadn't come up with the two-book technique, simultaneously reading one book in his right hand and one in his left, he wouldn't have got anywhere.

It occurred to him that he might appear pitiful. After he had been living in North London bookshops for four years, subsisting on reviews and marrying Japanese women who wanted nationality lifts, although he felt fine, he could see that people might think spending your whole life in either bookshops or libraries was wretched. He decided he couldn't spend all his time in bookshops in North London since he didn't want his horizons stunted. So he started touring: France, Germany and finally America.

What had he learned so far? Motion looks like progress. German bookshops had champagne, but only in American bookshops could you get frappachino. And hope. Hope. Books were made of hope, not paper. Hope that someone would read your book; that it would change the world or improve it; hope that people would agree with you, hope that people might believe you; hope that you'll be remembered, celebrated, hope that people would feel something. Hope that you would learn something; hope that you'll entertain or impress; hope you'll catch some cash; hope that you'll be proved right and hope that you'll be proved wrong.

Unfortunately there was the problem that even if you read everything, you don't read it as the same person. When he first read the *Iliad*, the opening was just the opening: an explanation. The anger of Achilles: people always thought it referred to Achilles' rage at losing his favourite slave-girl, or losing his sidekick Patroclus.

When he had read it first at eleven, he hadn't read it. At seventeen when he reapplied it was beginning to come into focus.

Yet only when he was thirty and he had been stuck in a lift, and he had gone in for the third time, had the meaning dripped through like portly rain drops infiltrating a roof.

It was no accident that the first word in Western literature was anger. Achilles' anger. He now saw it was anger at being alive, anger at having no choice. The *Iliad* was the truth, the *Odyssey* the sales brochure, where you dally with tricky women, get home and slaughter all the people who have been giving you grief. The *Iliad* was the scoop: stuck in a war you didn't ask for, working with chumps who couldn't even find Troy in the first place, unable to forget that your mother left you and that a centaur made you eat entrails, no choice, no challenge and the knowledge that you're not going home and that nothing is going to make you feel better.

When he read reports of spree-killers topping themselves he saw it wasn't because of remorse or desire to dodge the penal system, but despair because their actions hadn't made them feel any better, that they had leapt over the edge and the anger was still there. And it ran all the way through. Gilgamesh was angry. Jahweh was angry. Moses was angry. Pharaoh was beside himself. Electra was incandescent. Oedipus frothing. The Ronin was hopping mad. Hamlet was miffed. Orlando was furioso.

The problem was Upstairs. Karma. Kismet. Destiny. Fate. The Fates. Parcae. Namtar. The Norns. Doom. Fortune. Providence. Luck. Cosmo. Allah. Book of Fate. Threads. The words turned up again and again; they were the clichés he read over and over, not because the writers were unimaginative but because there was no other way of putting it.

Fulhams were what you got. The dice were loaded, but you had to throw them to see how the numbers fell.

He strolled to the Barnes & Noble on Union Square.

Generally the bigger they were, the easier it was. You found a quiet stretch of shelving just before closing time and made yourself scarce, until everyone had gone and you could get bookcrunching. He hadn't been caught very often. Over the years he had only been apprehended four times and had been let off.

They had looked at him in a way he didn't like to think

about, which suggested that he was either a failed burglar who couldn't get it right, or too failed an individual to want to be close to. Only the woman in Nuneaton had called the police. "I'm calling the police", she had hissed. He could have easily have run off but he waited, not understanding why the woman had said that since if he had been possessed of criminal intent or a guilty conscience it would have primed him to get going or to get ugly. He hadn't run off, chiefly, because he had had nowhere to run to. He had read twenty pages of *North and South* before the constabulary showed up. They weren't able to get very excited with no sign of damage, forced entry or theft. "We'll say no more about it this time", one said, since there really was nothing more to say.

It was not being prepared, you would fumble for a sentence in your pocket and come out with what was there or carry on fumbling. Walking home from school when he was eleven, two girls his age whom he had noticed regularly walking home the other way on the other side of the street, crossed over:

"Is it okay if I hit you?" the blonde had asked. He had been thinking about the question and an answer, when the blonde's fist impacted unpleasantly on his jaw. He then thought what he should do. He smiled and walked away.

Without preparation, it was sticky. In Portland once, he had been deep into Phlegon of Tralles' *Book of Marvels* and the Emperor Hadrian's centaur, so engrossed and not expecting anything since it was a humid summer two o'clock in the morning, sleepy in a sleepy town, that he hadn't registered another presence in the bookshop.

His attention was disturbed by the owner, a large man clutching a camp bed, pleading not to be killed. "Please don't kill me", the owner repeated sinking to his knees; puzzling, since he was only armed with a 215-page paperback and the incident with the girl had taught him he didn't have a fearsome aspect.

"The air conditioning packed up at home. It's just too hot.

I have money here, I'll show you. I won't tell the Police anything. Just let me live." He had wanted to roll out his standard story of having been accidentally locked in, but he never had been any better at lying than he had been at telling the truth, and the owner was having none of it. Taking the money was the easiest option, so he did and went to a hotel with enough books to get himself through the next day. He could see how he might be perceived as criminal, but he couldn't fathom how he had made it to dangerous; the incident left him splattered with interestingness and power.

As Barnes & Noble closed, he hunkered down in Politics and waited an hour for the building to clear of sounds. There had never been a book that hadn't contained fibres of other books; to write you have to read first. Could he be a person that had nothing of others in him? Was there anyone else who worried about no one eating fish in the *Iliad*? And who remembered the thirty-three terms of abuse for tax collectors gathered by Pollux of Naucrates? At the same time wondering if Apuleius' lost novel *Hermagoras* would ever turn up? While not forgetting to ponder if the *De Tribus Impostoribus Mundi* had ever existed?

He then made for the luxurious armchair that had endeared Barnes & Noble to him so much and plunged into (on the right) *Singularly Deluded* and (on the left) *The World's Desire*.

He got tired of it sometimes, but he kept going because he had gone too far to go back. A bout of weakness had made him take a job for two months, but it hadn't made things better.

His concentration couldn't have been that good because he heard coughing. For a few moments he sat motionless as if that might change something. Faintly, he detected it again. He thought about letting coughing be coughing, but couldn't get back into left or right.

Reluctantly investigating, on the first floor, he could see a thin woman dressed in mixed black. Attractive. He knew she wasn't staff, he was familiar with the assistants and also she had an . . . unstaffy manner. She was reading.

Not only was she reading intently, but she held a book in her left hand, and another in her right.

His steps startled her. Promptly, she closed the books, and slotted them back into the shelves. "You must be closing", she said in an appealing way. Her skin was pale, her lips gotcha red.

He wanted to say that he didn't work there.

"Don't look at me that way", she snapped.

She set the alarms off as she left.

He concluded that he felt okay but he feared he would feel bad, and that the badness was on its way.

November 27, 1998

Cheers

By Helen Simpson

The frost which beautified the car that morning had turned it into something else, a hardened glacé fruit, the green of its paintwork obscured by a nap of crystal bristles. Inside, Lois tried the ignition a few more times and tutted at the engine's croupy yelping.

When she looked up at passing cars, she saw dazzled faces screwed into eyeless masks. The forecast had promised a windchill factor of minus twelve in the week to come. She couldn't get it to start so she would have to walk to the station.

All across Cator Park trees stood cold and fabulous, elaborately naked in their diamonds. Crack troops flashing silver from the windows of nearby houses charged into their leafless branches and ended up in smithereens. Lois stalked along the paths like a film star, collar up and hands thrust deep in pockets.

On the station platform she stood beneath a sweet and heartless blue sky with no warmth or depth to it. It would be much easier to live if it were always like this, thought Lois: thin-blooded, energetic, unsmudged. The other sort of December day – defeated outlook, wet pavements, fine mean sleet – was harder to take.

Once on the London Bridge train she opened that morning's Christmas cards, a batch of wassail cups and donkeys and gaitered snowballers, and studied the hand-written messages inside. So Isobel had got her divorce after all. And here was Sally announcing that she and Gavin and their brood were moving to the country. On the whole Lois thought this was a mistake which would lead to an increase in their morosity and paranoia. They were trying to twitch their coat hems away from the rest of humanity, and would spend their whole time in the car listening to story tapes. The main thing, thought Lois, looking out of the window at south London's back gardens, the important thing as middle age came and sat down on you with its enormous bum, the vital thing surely was, not to grow too careful of yourself.

She reviewed her arrangements for the rest of that day. The three boys were at her childminder's and would stay overnight as she, Lois, was meeting an old college friend for a meal after the shops closed, and would be late back. And William could no longer be asked to do anything domestic like collect the children. His home was now less his castle than his garage.

In the last year he had been coming home later and later until it hardly seemed worth it, with eyes like fried eggs, completely unreachable, falling half-clothed dead asleep beside her. He wouldn't say what it was, if it was anything worse than not being young any more. He wouldn't talk to her. Last night she had seen by the landing light how he lay with his mouth half-open, a little pocket of rotten-fruit breath playing at its entrance, and she had been tempted to light a match a couple of inches above his teeth and watch the ghostly blue flames dance over his features.

At London Bridge she went underground, resurfacing at Oxford Circus on a wave of close-packed shoppers. Jammed together like this, sharing each other's warm and stale breath, shoulder against back or arm or ribcage, each struggled to preserve some inner distance by refusing to meet other eyes. I like being among people and not knowing them, even this, thought Lois; I like being part of the crowd. She surged across Oxford Street on another wave, then expertly up the escalators in John Lewis until she stood at a shelf of bolts of plastic-coated fabric. Cosiness was the worst of the Christmas cons, she decided as she rejected the Dingley Dell design.

Two metres should do it, she thought, examining the other

patterns, envisaging her dining table with the extra leaf in it at two o'clock on Christmas Day. There was William at the head, well into the next bottle, blearily inaccessible. Beside him sat his mother, chatting her way round the orbital loop of early Alzheimer's. Then there were the three boys, rolling sprouts at each other and at their cousins; and her younger sister, widowed that year, still electric with grief and terror; her elder sister, not even trying to look as though she were not hungering after her unfortunately married man at the head of his own groaning festive board; and their angry mother, sixty-eight, mouth stained with red wine, like a pike in claret.

"Two and a half metres please", she said, as the man unwound a panorama of wipe-clean poinsettias. There they had all been, ready at the gates when she had woken early that morning, waiting to walk right into her mind and sit down and let her look after them. Beneath her duvet she had felt herself unravelled by rancorous pity, dismembered by tenderness and resentment.

The rest of the afternoon went in packed shops and glitter and cash. She had seen it all before, she knew just where to go and what to buy, but it still delighted her, choosing presents, because she was good at it. She was looking forward to seeing Holly too. She loved being out, talking about something outside herself. They were meeting in a Polish café Holly had chosen.

This café, Lois found, as she later consulted her map of the Underground, was four stops down the Bakerloo line then five along District and Circle. Once on the train she sat discrete and silent beneath her carrier bags. Christmas had become one big advertising campaign for the family, but nobody pointed out how the family would close you down to the outside world given half a chance. She glanced appreciatively at the strangers around her, all ages and shapes and sizes.

There were faces foolish from office parties, and late guarded shoppers like herself. Beside her a tall black man sat reading an evangelical newsletter, while members of the

Japanese family opposite were examining a programme for *The Phantom of the Opera*.

At the head of the gangway swayed a frisky grizzled growler and crooner. He was conducting his own party, growing livelier by the minute. Now he was creeping up to women sitting alone, a Rumpelstiltskin on pointed toes of stealth, thrusting out his chin and snorting a whisky-drenched blast into their faces, laughing with delight when they jumped. He did it to Lois and in spite of herself she jumped like the rest. Next he skipped over to the Japanese family and stood there in front of them making slitty eyes and hooting with pleasure.

Lois smelt the whisky which fuelled him, and considered the old theory of spontaneous combustion. His every organ must be saturated with Scotch, his veins running amber, his bodily tissues highly inflammable. The world was awash on a sea of alcohol, she realized, Russia, Scotland, Romania, the entire Eastern Bloc. Oh, and Scandinavia too, of course, its length and breadth, and don't forget the Low Countries.

Tired of teasing, he lurched across the carriage to a support rail against which he steadied himself, then took out a cigarette. Lois held her breath as he lit it with a clumsily struck match.

"There is no smoking on the Underground trains", came a voice sumptuous in its gravity.

It was the man beside her who had spoken.

Lois nearly jumped out of her skin. The rest of the carriage leant forward agog. The drunk narrowed his eyes incredulously at his challenger, then opened them clownishly wide, then narrowed them again.

"You must put out your cigarette", said her neighbour.

When the drunk took a defiant drag and puffed smoke at him like a naughty boy, he rose from his seat, plucked out the cigarette between finger and thumb, and ground it underfoot. Then he sat down and resumed reading his Christian news.

Lois caught a cunning look on the drinker's face. She watched his hand creep towards the inside pocket of his mac in elaborate slow motion; as if, she thought, for a knife.

She got up and moved away and murmured her worry about the knife to the young Australian she found herself standing beside. No, he said, there's no knife, and anyway he's a big guy, he can take care of himself. But sheer bone and heft are no protection against steel, she thought, uneasy as the train at last drew in at Piccadilly Circus. The drinker darted up to his reprover and shook his hand as though they were old friends, unleashing as he did so some incomprehensible truism about life, or death; then nipped off the train at the last minute with a merry farewell wave of his hand.

Every woman who left the train after that made a point of sidling past the hero on her way out and muttering some praise or thanks. He acknowledged each tribute with a nod, and continued to read. Lois, who had gone back to her seat, turned to him and murmured that it had been brave of him but shouldn't he be careful in case of a knife? He turned and looked at her with unsmiling eyes.

"Someone has to stand up and say it", he said.

"I suppose so . . .", she began.

"There is too much freedom", he told her, closing down the conversation.

Too much freedom, she thought, as she changed trains at Embankment. Too much freedom! That's not the sort of moral you want to hear. Not from a hero.

Holly was already at a corner table sipping from a litre of Bulgarian red when Lois appeared with her shopping.

"There was a drunk on the train", began Lois, struggling out of her coat.

"All those ossif parties", said Holly. "I hate it when they vomit and you still have several stops to go. Let me pour you a glass."

"Cheers", said Lois. "Are your sixth-formers coming in with hangovers?" "Fourth-years up", said Holly. "I think we should give them compulsory lines in December. Write out a hundred times, I must drink a pint of milk before I go down the pub."

"Or they could choose instead: Never drink when you're angry, lonely, tired, hungry or bored."

"So, never", said Holly. "Basically. Cheers."

"They'll all be at raves soon", said Lois, raising her glass. "Safe from the Demon Drink."

"Red wine is good for you", said Holly as she glugged away. "Although it has to be at least four units a day before there's any effect on the bad-cholesterol lipoproteins."

"I needed that", said Lois. "This sentimental line on the family they trot out every Christmas, it makes me angry; as though there's some transformative magic wood."

"I blame Dickens", said Holly. "The memory of sorrow softens the heart. Does it hell."

"Such cosiness", Lois hissed, glaring at the menu. "Such lies. I can't think of a single family that isn't dysfunctional in some way. That's what they're for."

They studied the list, its barschst, its stuffed cabbage in white sauce and its meat balls in red.

"I'm ravenous", said Holly "Meatballs for me. I've come straight from a very long Nativity play. Dave's youngest was a shepherd."

"The boys had theirs yesterday", said Lois. "You know the bit when there's no room at the inn? They said: Unfortunately everywhere was fully booked."

"How very Sydenham", said Holly. "We don't get that sort of language out in Ilford."

They ate and drank and discussed Holly's plans to abandon teaching and go into computer programming. Although she thought this might drive her mad with boredom, it would pay enough to enable her and her partner Dave to move out of her flat and into a house; and since Dave's children were staying most weekends now this had its advantages. His wife still would not give him a divorce. His children blamed her, Holly, for their parents' separation. She and Dave wanted their own baby but she had had a miscarriage last year and time was running out. Meanwhile her father's second wife had left him a couple of weeks ago and he too would be coming to Holly's for Christmas.

Lois listened to more about Dave's vile wife, his malevolent children, about how it was Dave's duty to himself they were ignoring, and noticed how this always happened with Holly now after the first few drinks. She lost her honesty. She would look at the complicated and painful equation she and Dave had had to draw up in order to be together, then she would have another drink and boldly claim the moral high ground as well. This was all done in what Lois privately called Polonius-speak.

"What do you think?" asked Holly at last, staring at her with a certain loss of focus.

"I'm on the side of love and happiness", said Lois tactfully.

"So how's William these days?" asked Holly, ordering another half-litre of wine without reference to Lois.

"I don't really know", said Lois. "He's stopped talking to me and he's drinking too much."

"Make him say limericks", said Holly with relish, then attempted the one about round the rugged rock but fell at the third syllable.

Lois watched her heaving with giggles and realized almost casually that William had borrowed more money from somewhere, without telling her, and had lost it again. That was why he could not talk to her. Her thoughts strode ahead of her in seven-league boots.

By the end of the meal Holly had drunk a good deal. Her eyes looked skew-whiff, as though they were trying to regroup on the same side of her nose, like a flounder. She was challenging Lois's memory as to the origins of English carols, which had been the subject of a college essay they had both tackled twenty years ago. It was hot chocolate then, thought Lois.

"Lullay, lullay", sang Holly, causing heads to turn. "Thou little tiny child . . ." and her voice cracked and her face weakly crumbled.

"It's that tune", she whispered as Lois hastily paid the bill and passed her tissues under the table.

Oh hell, thought Lois, Oh bloody hell, while trying to hail a taxi and reassure her that nobody had noticed.

"I'll be all right", mumbled red-eyed Holly, tripping over a carrier bag. "Got a return ticket."

"Ilford please", said Lois, giving her a cross hug and bundling her into the back of a black cab, countering the driver's obvious lack of enthusiasm for his fare with a twenty pound note up front.

"She all right then?" said the driver, casting a leery look over his shoulder at the figure slumped across the back seat.

"Of course she's all right", snapped Lois, slamming the door. "She's a teacher."

The trains were in chaos that night but she took one as far as Lewisham, then caught a bus which was destined eventually to pass through Lower Sydenham. She even had a seat on the end of the three-person banquette behind the driver, with a large sleepy woman lolling between her and the man at the other end.

"Stay awake", said the man now and then into the sleepy woman's ear. When he stood up to get off the bus at the corner of Catford Road, the woman tottered after him and crashed to the pavement. That seemed to rouse her a little, and she looked up into the bus with a puzzled expression and said, "Drummond Road?" "She's not with me", called the man to the driver. "Says her stop's Drummond Road."

"Anybody getting off at Drummond Road might see this lady right?" called the driver down the bus into the crowd of blank embarrassed faces.

Oh bloody hell, thought Lois.

"I am", she said grimly, helping haul the woman back on. Her black tights had split into a web of white holes and wet red knees.

"Shorry darling", the woman slurred, and slumped

against her on the seat and fell asleep.

"Wake up", said Lois. "What's your name?"

"Treesa", mumbled the woman. "Tess. Tess."

"Come on Tess. It's our stop next. Drummond Road."

"Drummond Road", said Tess sitting up, eyes closed.

"You be all right then?" said the bus driver as Lois, festooned with carrier bags, helped her down.

"I don't know, do I", snapped Lois, followed through the window by thirty pairs of eyes as the bus drove off.

"Drummond Road", she said loudly. "What NUMBER. Stay awake!" "Hundred shirty sor. Shirty sick", said Tess, fishing out an enormous bunch of keys and handing them over. Her eyes were closing again.

"A hundred and thirty-four?" shouted Lois. "Thirty-six?" "Kiss", said Tess with a great effort. "Shirty kiss. Hunnard shirty kiss."

"A hundred and thirty-SIX?" "Us", said Tess exhaustedly. She was wearing stilettoes, which made her lurch fearsomely, but she would not take them off.

"Keep going", said Lois through gritted teeth. It was like coaxing along a giant toddler.

At number a hundred and thirty-six she tried every key on the bunch without success. She pressed the seven doorbells in turn, but nobody answered. She tried the keys again. On the second time round the lock gave and they were in. Tess led the way up the carpetless stairs and as Lois followed her she glimpsed one of the downstairs lodgers open his door a crack. She saw a slice of face, the glitter of an eye, and then the crack closed noiselessly.

"Smine", said Tess, indicating a door on the landing. Then she went into the lavatory beside it and bolted herself in.

"Oh bloody hell", said Lois, putting down her carrier bags and going through the business with the keys again, twice, because this door had two separate locks. It opened at last.

"Are you all right in there?" she called through the bolted door.

"I'm grand, darling", came the voice, with effortful enunciation. "Don't you worry about me then."

"But you'll come out in a minute?" called Lois.

"Sure I will, baby."

Lois picked up her bags and pushed her way into the room. There was a brown-sheeted bed with clothes heaped all over it and round it on the floor. The kitchen sink in the corner held underwear soaking in a plastic washing-up bowl, a wooden spoon sticking out as though to stir it. There was nothing else except two Christmas cards above the blocked-in fireplace, and a huge bare fir tree which almost touched the ceiling.

Lois rinsed the cups and mugs on the draining board, filled them with cold water and set them up by the bed. She held her breath and emptied the underwear into the sink, then put the bowl down by the bed too. Next she pleaded and bullied through the bolted door for the woman to come out.

"All right, darling", came the reply in conciliatory tones. "All right. I'll get you something to eat, baby. Can I get you something to eat?" "But first of all you must come out", begged Lois. "Please."

The woman said she loved her, and offered to feed her again. Lois leant against the wall and closed her eyes.

"Please come out", she repeated. She was nearly finished. She had had enough.

The door rattled open at last, with Tess emerging like a big shamed child, clutching more underwear.

"It's all right", clucked Lois, faint with relief. "Don't worry. It doesn't matter."

"I'm shorry, darling", moaned Tess. "I'm shorry shorry."

The vulnerability of this big soft woman, her gaping handbag, her bunch of keys so readily handed over and really the lack of fight in her, made Lois think back almost with nostalgia to the spiteful goblin on the train. She helped Tess on to the bed, where she curled in a foetal hump and, growling, pulled the covers tightly over her head.

Lois stepped back to the door and realized she was holding her breath. The main thing now was to leave Tess inside the room, with her handbag and keys beside her; and for her, Lois, to be outside the room, with her carrier bags, pulling the door shut. This she managed. Her heart was thumping hard with tiredness and uselessness and she clumped down the hollow stairs as fast as she could, with a panicky apprehension on her way out that she would have to pass a wolf at the door.

Outside in the cold she felt safe again. She walked on for a while past kebab bars and minicab offices, then noticed a riproaring bevy of boys at the next pub, and decided to turn off the main road. The side streets would be a quieter route home, even if they took longer. In their tiny front gardens ivy leaves had been chilled to shagreen, and all the leaves on the privet hedges were pewter-plated. That's what I want, she thought; I want to be pewter-plated.

The curtains in this road had mostly been left undrawn, and at nearly every window glowed a well-lit tree in a darkened room. When she got home she would open the front door and the first thing she saw would be the tree she and the boys had decorated two days ago. She was very tired. She trudged on under the street lamps. Safe as houses. Safe as trees. Sane as trees. Mad as trees. Why had Tess dragged that mad great tree up into her room? What business had a tree inside a house anyway? You shouldn't let trees indoors, they belonged outside.

The house would go too, that was it. And he couldn't tell her. Bloody hell, she thought, stopping in her tracks. Why couldn't he tell me that before, she wondered. I know why, he thinks it's a competition and he's failed. So that's what it is, she thought, relieved after all the silence; though of course it was terrible. Better out than in, though. So to speak. She stood heaving gale-force sighs and shaking her head.

A church clock struck the hour, lengthily. It was midnight. She heard the chugging past of a distant night bus, and laughter from people leaving a house further along the road. When she looked up at the roofs of the houses she saw there was a white velvet pelt of frost on the tiles, just as there was on the slats of the garden fences. This frost glittered superbly in the glow from the street lamps.

A forest of trees stood shining in their front-room havens, winking their fairy lights at her as she stood out on the pavement. Round the rugged rock the ragged rascal ran. The rooms which sheltered them would be balmy with spice, evergreen and zest. In the light of their beauty she felt a kick of stubborn happiness as well as everything else. She blew her nose like a trumpet. Then she picked up her carrier bags of presents one by one, and set off on the rest of the walk home.

December 25, 1998

Annals of the
Honorary Secretary

By James Lasdun

It isn't known when Lucille Thomas first appeared among us.
Who brought her, or at least told her where our circle met,
remains equally mysterious. One or two members have
claimed the distinction, but with little to offer yet in the way of
evidence. Most of her casual remarks from the period before
her first performance have passed into oblivion; those that sur-
vive have the over-cherished lustre of apocrypha.

The consensus is that she had been coming to our meetings
for perhaps as long as a year before she made her debut.
During that time she maintained an attitude of more or less
silent watchfulness. I don't recall her asking anything during
question times, or taking the opportunity during our less
formal discussions, to advertise herself by saying something
clever or controversial.

I myself had taken little notice of her until just a few days
before her first performance, when certain familiar signs – a
definite concentration of purpose visible in the outward
manner; a sudden close interest in matters of procedure –
suggested to me the imminent breaking of a silence.

At that time we were meeting at the Kurwens' house up
near the North Circular. The large double drawing-room was
crowded with people standing in groups or sitting on the
Kurwens' velour chairs and sofas. We had just listened to a
talk and there was the usual murmur of discussion. I was
sitting between Brenda and Stewart Kurwen and I remember
gesturing towards the back of the room where Lucille, as yet

unknown to us, sat on the window seat, and saying that I thought we would be hearing from her before long.

"Good, good", Brenda said. "Any idea who she is?" "No."

Stewart took his pipe from his mouth and smiled. "All the better."

There was nothing unusual in our not knowing the woman's name. Our doors have always been open to any individual who cares to join us. The perplexing and often tedious nature of our presentations tends to put off all but the kind of people whom we would welcome anyway. Occasionally a charlatan has tried to impose on us, usually in the hope of attracting the attention of one of our patrons. Most people, however, come in good faith, and we have never felt a need to regulate our membership with formalities of introduction or recommendation.

The Kurwens and I looked across the room at the young woman. She was sipping coffee with the cup and saucer held close to her lips as if she were nervous of spilling it on the carpet. Behind her slightly bulbous head the afternoon light showed her untidy brown hair to be thin, and emphasized the irregularities of her long, bony face. Quite a few similar-looking young women and men have passed through our doors over the years (I was one myself), and there was nothing to suggest that this one would turn out to be any different from the general type – sober and serious, not gifted, but educated enough to make a useful contribution.

On a Saturday afternoon in October, I took the Tube to Bounds Green station and walked from there to the Kurwens' house. It was a cold, damp day, and the long residential streets were lifeless except for the occasional coloured flicker of a television screen in a front window. I remember a melancholy feeling from the dreariness of the walk, the brackish sky, and the smell of new, wet asphalt.

There were perhaps twenty people in the drawing-room; not a bad turnout for a rainy afternoon. Most of the older crowd were there – Ellen Crowcroft, Marc and Sabine

Chenier, Janice Hall, the Kurwens of course. No doubt like me they had made the effort out of courtesy for a newcomer: it had been announced that the young woman, Lucille Thomas, was going to make her debut.

I sat in an armchair next to Ellen Crowcroft. She had put her hearing aid in for the occasion, and was wearing face powder, grains of which were visible in the wrinkles around her chin. On the other side of me – in a row of wooden chairs, were several younger people who seemed to know each other. Ellen turned to me, her large, asthmatic chest heaving a little wheezily under her dress.

"New blood tonight", she whispered, and we shared the sceptical but ever-hopeful smile of a pair of old-timers.

The clock over the raised platform at the end of the room struck four. This was the official starting time, but as always we waited a few minutes for latecomers. A pale, wintry light came through the bay windows, lying with a hard gleam on the Kurwens' ornate coffee urn, beside which stood rows of green cups and saucers.

Trevor McWilliam, who was giving the first presentation, sat on a chair in the front row, shuffling through his papers. He was a self-effacing man who had been with us for several years. He wasn't gifted, but his theoretical work was usually interesting, even if it tended more to consolidate ground already covered than actually to take us forward in our investigations.

In the same row, separated by five or six empty chairs, sat Lucille. She didn't appear to have papers or any other equipment with her. I assumed this meant she was going to extemporize a talk, and I remember feeling anxious on her behalf.

Stewart Kurwen strolled to the front of the room, puffing at his pipe.

"I think we might as well begin", he said.

Trevor spoke for an hour. As ever, his presentation was scholarly, a little meandering, with one or two pedantic jokes which we laughed at dutifully. Some of our members, who were following his researches more closely than I was, jotted things down in notebooks as he read. I myself was content to sit and let my thoughts wander where they chose: at a certain point one comes to recognize the limitations of a person's mind, and in a general if not a literal way, one knows in advance what they are going to say on any given subject.

There was a short question-and-answer period. Stewart Kurwen stepped up to the platform again, thanked Trevor, and gave a few words of welcome to the newcomer, Lucille Thomas, who was to follow him. Evidently Stewart had no more idea what to expect than the rest of us, and after extending good wishes and appreciation on behalf of us all, he smiled at the young woman and led us in the round of applause with which we customarily welcome a debut.

The young woman climbed onto the platform and stood at the very front of it, ignoring both the chair and the lectern. It had grown quite dark in the room by now. The lamp on the platform was behind her, filling the irregular hollows of her cheeks and eyes with shadow.

There was a pronounced hush in the audience, as there always is when someone takes the stage for the first time. This is a moment of hope and excitement for us all. However much experience may have taught us to expect disappointment or at best qualified success, the mere impression of possibility, of promise not yet unfulfilled, tends to fill even the most jaded of us with a sense of impending revelation.

"I'm just going to stand here", Lucille said.

She stood at the front of the platform with her hands at her side, her jacket hanging shabbily over her thin-looking torso, her hair hanging in lank clusters. It dawned on us that her presentation was going to be practical, not theoretical, and at once the already quite keen attentiveness of the audience became even sharper. The proportion of people who are actually gifted (or believe they are) to those of us who are merely curious and enthusiastic, is of course tiny, and "practical" demonstrations are correspondingly rare. Not only that; most of them fail, whether because of unreadiness, self-delusion, loss of nerve, or simply through some delicate imbalance in the atmosphere.

In a very short time, however, it was apparent that this presentation was not going to join the list of failures. Quite how the terms of its success were to be judged was less certain (they are still being debated), but nobody could doubt that something extraordinary was happening, and within seconds I think we all realized we were in the presence of a virtuoso.

Words didn't enter into Lucy's presentation, and words probably will not convey the experience any better, say, than the bundles of triple zeros in an astronomy book convey the physical dimensions of space.

Ellen Crowcroft, most simply and perhaps most accurately, said that as she sat watching the girl, she had suddenly started to feel as if she were dying. Janice Hall said that it reminded her of a morning when she had woken from a blissful dream and had lain for several seconds bathed in its ebbing light, until, with an overwhelming feeling of desolation, she was left with the stark memory that her husband had left her the week before and was not coming back. In general we all felt it to be an experience of unillusion rather than the reverse. Some felt little more than the kind of lowering of spirits that a drink can easily remedy. One of the younger members reported feeling suicidal. A man whose name I don't know said that he had been reminded of the radiation therapy he had once been given for a tumour: a similar distressing sense of prematurely surrendering the integrity of one's living flesh to a force from the inorganic universe; the same feelings of acute, unnameable anguish and danger. Personally what I remember is this: first an abrupt transition from wondering what the young woman on the plat-form was going to do, into a realization that I was being acted upon by a power outside my own control. Next, a feeling of being very quickly drained of energy: a sensation of heaviness in my limbs, of torpid fatigue in my eyes and head. Then, for about a minute, an almost dizzying sadness, as if some mysterious essence that made life tolerable was sluicing out of me. Finally I just felt numb and inert; incurious about myself, the girl on stage, and the people around me.

I left directly the demonstration was over: I had recovered from my numbness sufficiently to be extremely perturbed by what had happened, and I wanted to reflect on its implications in peace. I walked to the Tube station along the same streets that earlier on had struck me as so oppressively dull and repetitive. This time though, presumably as a physiological reaction to what I had just experienced, these houses, the lamp-posts, the pillar boxes, clipped laurel hedges, creosoted fences, cherry trees, cars, pigeons, brackish dusk, bloated clouds, and disappearing sun, impinged on me in a quite different light, a light of delicate and mysterious enchantment, as if my relation of them had been subtly shifted so as to reveal animating nuances of shade and depth that had previously been invisible to me. A sensation of calm happiness spread through me; warm, comforting, and expansive. I went home with the feeling of excitement that accompanies the realization, so rare as one gets older, that one has just been shown something absolutely new.

Lucille repeated the demonstration several times for us over the next few weeks. Word spread, and with every performance the Kurwens' double drawing-room became more crowded. Each time, the same annihilating pall fell over the hushed audience within a few seconds of the girl taking the platform. The same palpable sensations of energy being depleted, of depression, listlessness and apathy being uncovered like successive archaeological strata under a sharp and probing excavating tool, were reported in discussion afterwards. Few of us were in any doubt that something of profound importance was being revealed. What was it though? From the answers Lucille gave to our questions, it was apparent that she didn't understand her gift any more than we did.

Certainly it didn't seem to give her any pleasure or pride. On the platform she merely stood still; stooped, slightly derelict-looking, staring at the floor with her hands hanging limply at her sides. Afterwards she looked and sounded if anything even more despondent than she had before. She seemed to offer herself as the victim of an unknown sickness offers herself for examination to a group of physicians; not so much in the hope of being cured, as of redeeming an otherwise pointless suffering from futility by giving it at least the potential usefulness of medical data.

One day – it must have been Lucille's fourth or fifth performance – Stewart Kurwen announced that she was going to do something different this time, and wanted us to stand closely around her so that we could see.

She sat on a chair at the edge of the platform. There must have been more than fifty of us: the full complement of members, including ones who had not been seen for several years. With some difficulty we crowded into a circle on the floor in front of her and the platform behind. A single recessed ceiling light was left on, dropping a beam directly on to Lucille. One of her hands was balled into a fist, and after we had all settled into positions where we could see clearly, she put her arm out, propping it on a crossed knee, and opened the fist.

In the palm of her hand was what looked at first like a shred of whiteish dust, but on closer inspection turned out to be a little downy feather; no more than an inch long, with a needle-thin white spine out of which grew first a nimbus of fluff, and then, for about a third of an inch, neatly tapering white filaments clinging to each other with their minute jelly-ish barbules to form a triangular tip. Certainly it looked closely related to dust, and by that branch of the family a cousin of absolute nothingness. But obviously the whole of creation stands between this latter pair, and most of evolution between the former, and for all its frailty and insubstantiality, the little feather's involvement with existence was tight and intricate. I emphasize this because as it began to disappear under our eyes, melting away gradually but steadily from the outer fringes, what we experienced was not the pleasing but almost insignificant difference between its being in the palm of Lucille's hand, and its not being there, that would have been produced by a purely aesthetic perception of the disappearance, but a feeling of something quite powerfully discomforting, both physically and, for want of a better word, ethically; as if in standing around Lucille we had come under the stress of some immense accelerative or centrifugal force, and from the thickened continuum of space between ourselves and the surrounding objects, something was being torn with a savage and stupendous violence.

Two or three more frail things passed into nothingness under Lucille's impassive gaze that winter: a dead bluebottle, a hairpin, a tiny sprig of evergreen leaves – these latter apparently involving more effort than she had expected; after beginning to fade at their outer edges, they started tremulously recovering their shape instead of disappearing, as if struggling to reassert themselves in defiance of whatever force Lucille was deploying against them. But after a few minutes they lost ground again, and this time steadily faded away.

Spring arrived, and with it our New Year's party. Following the practices of civilizations better versed in the rites of renewal and reinvigoration than our own (one thinks of the Persian Tatars, the Mandaeans of Iraq), we designate Spring Equinox as the first day of our collective calendar, and see it in each year with a party at the house of one of our patrons. While the taboos of our own civilization make an out-and-out orgy (the orthodox model for such festivities) problematic, we do all we can with food, drink, music and dancing to induce in ourselves at least an approximation of the state of *eudaimonia* considered necessary to the sacred moment.

This year the party was to be held at the house of Helen Van Kemp, a wealthy and generous widow in St John's Wood.

It was a cool, moist evening. I arrived at the gates of Mrs Van Kemp's mansion at the same time as Janice Hall, and I remember Janice remarking that you could smell spring in the air. Torches lined the short garden path, burning with flickering yellow flames. A maid took our coats and we stood a moment in front of the hallway mirror, checking our appearances. With the exception of a few theatrical types, our members tend not to be especially interested in sartorial matters, and to an outsider we would probably look a rather dowdy lot on most occasions. But for our New Year's party it was customary for everyone to dress up in whatever finery they possessed. For the men black tie or white tie, gold and crimson cummerbunds, war medals, silk cravats, and so on; for the women evening dresses, high heels, lipstick and perfume. Janice, I recall, was wearing a green dress of a demure but close-fitting cut that suited her surprisingly well. She had had her hair done in a new style that made her look younger, and she wore a pearl necklace with matching earrings. I was reminded of how attractive she had always seemed to me when she had first joined us, long before her husband had left her and a kind of determined shabbiness set in, as if she were trying retroactively to rationalize his unexpected rejection of her. I told her she looked very elegant, and she thanked me, smiling at me in the mirror.

Helen Van Kemp came along a corridor to greet us in her usual effusively considerate manner. Like many very rich people, she worked hard at making one feel like an old and particularly dear friend from whom only the most extraordinary circumstances had kept her away in the interval that had passed. Her connection with our group dated from ten or twelve years ago, when Ellen Crowcroft – at that time more active than she is today – had put her in touch several times with her husband, Sir Clyde, who had been killed when his private jet crashed over the Isle of Man. I myself was present at the last of these occasions; it was spectacular and intensely moving. After twenty minutes or so the candlelit room filled suddenly with an overpowering smell of jet fuel. We were all terrified the place was going to explode. An ecstatic-looking spasm seized Ellen. She tilted back her neck, and out of her radiantly smiling lips came the voice of a man – muffled a little as if by static, but perfectly intelligible, and with a kind of clipped, raffish tenderness that brought us all rapidly to tears. "Helen darling", it said, "I'm here. You're much missed. I can't stay. Think of me always." That's all. Ellen wouldn't accept payment herself, and instead suggested Mrs Van Kemp become a patron of our group, which she very willingly did. Since then she has funded the researches of a number of our more promising younger members, and more than once taken her turn hosting our New Year's party.

This one was already in full swing. Janice and I followed Helen into the suite of grand rooms, some of them partially cleared for dancing. There was a wonderfully festive atmosphere. A jazz band corralled in potted palms was playing dance music. Many members had brought their families or other guests: children in fancy dress were running around; white-gloved waiters were threading through garrulous clusters with trays of champagne. Buffet tables laden with salmon, cold sirloin, breads, salads, fruit tarts, and other desserts, had been set out in the dining room. All the rooms had been garlanded with spring flowers. Boughs of lilac and forsythia were arranged around the windows; daffodils, lilies-of-the-valley and hyacinths stood in vases, filling the rooms with the fresh smell of spring.

The old gang were all there – Stewart and Brenda Kurwen, the Cheniers with their shy twin daughters both in pink and white frocks, Ellen Crowcroft looking splendid in her white stole, leaning on a gnarled, silver-knobbed cane, her hearing aid gleaming in her ear more like some totemic ornament than a medical appliance. We stood together, chatting about the old days, and when we had eaten we took to the floor for an hour or so of spirited dancing.

At midnight we went into an upstairs room where seats had been arranged around a raised platform. Our way of thanking our benefactors for their support was to present them with a demonstration by one or other of our more gifted members. Braidism, demonstrations of ectenic force, "community of sensation" experiments, and so on, have always been popular on such occasions, and I suspect the atmosphere must resemble that of certain drawing-rooms in the last century when celebrity performers did the rounds with their table-tapping, invisible piano-playing and other tricks. Last year Ellen Crowcroft actually recreated an experiment that J. H. Petetin of the Lyons Medical Society had performed on Mme de St Paul in the 1890s when someone in another room – in our case our hostess – put different foods in her mouth, while Ellen, with the pleasant smile that always appeared on her face as she settled into a trance, called out peppermint, mayonnaise, raspberry vinegar, anchovy, and so on, with faultless accuracy.

Naturally we had chosen Lucille to represent us at this year's party. In doing so we were aware of departing from a tradition of festive, perhaps essentially trivial, demonstration, but it was obviously out of the question for us to put forward anyone else. Besides, our benefactress had heard about Lucille, and wanted to see her perform.

The revelation of any great gift always draws a wake of myth behind it as it settles into history. In Lucille's case, the mythologizing was in my view concurrent with the performance she proceeded to give. Confronted with things this strange and extreme, the mind tends, without realizing it, to translate what it beholds into terms more familiar to its own experience than those on which the phenomena themselves exist. In this case, since our perceptions were in themselves implicated in Lucille's performance, our sense of what actually happened must presumably be even further removed than usual from an "objective" memory. Furthermore, practically every one of us seems to have emerged with their own version of what happened, and while the gist of each version is the same, few of the details agree.

I myself, for example, remained unaware of most of the

physical occurrences reported by other witnesses. I didn't see the flowers wilt or the lilac and forsythia blossoms wither and blacken on their boughs. I was unaware of the carpet of mould spreading over the half-consumed dishes of food in the dining room. The apparently overpowering smells of rotten meat and mildew that some people remembered so vividly, didn't register with me at all. Nor did I observe the moths others saw massing in thick clusters on people's jackets and dresses. Although I would be the first to attribute these gaps in my testimony to the lack of a certain kind of receptiveness on my part, I remain convinced that what actually happened in that upstairs room was so far outside the experience of us all, that each of us was obliged to recreate it simultaneously in a kind of emergency cascade of metaphors.

What I do remember, aside from the immediate pandemonium that erupted when Lucille took the platform, and the sound of Mrs Van Kemp crying out for her to stop whatever it was she had started, was this: a feeling of bitter revulsion, directed both inward and outward; a sense of having partially disintegrated, putrefied even, and of being surrounded by a pack of horrifying, corpse-like beings. I remember looking at Stewart Kurwen, one of my oldest and dearest friends, with a feeling of sudden, overwhelming disgust, as if he had begun shamelessly decomposing before my eyes. Janice Hall, in whom earlier on I had noticed what seemed a resurgence of her youthful attractiveness, looked to me suddenly pallid, bloated and insubstantial, like some kind of fungal organism that would collapse in a puff of spores if you so much as touched it. Even her jewels seemed to have rotted, giving out not so much a gleam as a kind of phosphorescent glow. I recall vividly how the Chenier twins seemed to me for a moment like a pair of old crones dressed up in little pink and white frocks as though in a cadaverous mimicry of childhood. I pushed and clawed my way to the door along with everyone else, glimpsing Ellen Crowcroft turn and lunge back toward the darkness of the stage with a panicky cry of Lucille! Outside it was chilly and wet. The torches had gone out. A few people lingered near the entrance, but most of us went quickly off into the night, making our separate ways home.

As it happened, that presentation turned out to be the final act of Lucille's career, at least as far as her participation in our own circle was concerned. She never appeared at the Kurwens' house again. None of us knew where she lived, and since it is not our policy to solicit meetings or initiate searches of any kind, we refrained from any attempt to find her. We all, naturally, have our own surmises as to what became of her. Some of these are more extravagant than others. Personally I tend to believe that her powers simply burned themselves out in that moment of frantic brilliance. And rather than linger among us, watching us grow steadily disenchanted with her, she had the good sense to remove herself altogether from our midst. To use an analogy from poetry, her gift appeared to be lyric rather than epic, and like most lyric gifts, it was short-lived. On the other hand, the critical exegesis has only just begun.

January 29, 1999

Bosom Companions

By Dan Jacobson

My wife has left me, my children are grown up and live abroad, my business has been sold. I have not moved from the house I lived in when I was a husband, a father, a business-man, a semi-public figure. It is now much too big for me, but I have no intention of moving from it. A woman comes three times a week to do some cooking and cleaning; a gardener twice a month. For the rest I am left alone. I have no ambi-tions. I have no friends. It is a great relief to be answerable to no one. My mind is active, however. I read, I listen to music and cricket commentaries, go shopping, make notes of my dreams and thoughts. Occasionally I go to a club where I have a meal and play bridge with people I do not care about. My sister comes to see me from time to time or I pay a visit to her. She too lives alone now, and is hardly more sociable than I am. She says that there is much in her past life that she regrets; I tell her that my regrets all refer to the future. By that I chiefly mean the fear I have of illness and incapacity.

My sole companions are my dogs. There are three of them. No one but myself is ever allowed to feed them or groom them. They are wholly mine. I know it and they know it. Every morning and every evening we go out together on Hampstead Heath. For me – for them too, I am sure – it is the keenest pleasure of the day. We do the same circuit in all weathers and seasons: past the Highgate Ponds; up Parliament Hill, with its hazy or crystalline view of London's skyline; then north to Kenwood – and so home. Since they are closer to the ground than I am, and their senses are keener, the dogs probably know the slopes and tree-tufted crests of the circuit even more intimately than I do. They love to range beyond the limits of our route, though they seldom go so far astray as to lose sight of me. Or I of them.

They chase each other, bark at waterfowl on the ponds, make stiff-legged approaches to other dogs, and inspect closely every urinous and excremental trace that comes their way. They also take advantage of our outings to tend to their own needs: now squatting earnestly, necks stiff, eyes enlarged, hindquarters spread; now doing it on the trot – quite literally. Then they are off again. Sometimes, when I think I have lost them, mysterious shakings will convulse clumps of bracken or gorse nearby; then they emerge, snorting proudly, shaking their heads, jangling their collars. When we return to the roadway I call them together and reattach to their collars the leashes which I carry twisted around my hand and forearm like a set of phylacteries. They submit to this procedure without complaint.

We are soon home. The smallest of them, and the only bitch, is allowed into the house with me. The two others settle in their favourite positions in the garden, or stand outside the French windows of the living room, waiting with the incurable optimism and patience of their race for yet another outing to begin.

Now to distinguish between them. First, the mongrel, the (spayed) bitch, the runt of the pack. She has the body of a corgi, more or less, and the black and white patches of a fox terrier; a combination most people would find unappealing. Her coat is short, stiff and prickly. Being the smallest and weakest of them, it may be that she feels she must make an extra effort to keep her position in the household secure; hence the fawning affection towards me she always displays. She is a manic wriggler of her hindquarters; a lascivious licker of my hands, face and shoes; a slitherer towards me across polished floors. She is also the only one of the three who tries to stand upright: not by sitting back on her haunches, as many dogs do, but by rising as high as she can on her hind legs, in quasi-human fashion. To keep herself in this posture, she has to flay the air in front of her with forepaws, over and over again. The effort soon exhausts her. Then, as if with a mixture of pride in having tried so hard to compete with me, and rage at having failed, she jumps up at me, barking, whimpering, snapping her teeth, revealing the liverish spots that discolour her gums.

All I have to do to quieten her is to bend over, stroke her once or twice, and take her brief, oddly oblong muzzle in my hand. What ecstasies of grovelling follow! She rolls over on her back, displaying her pink belly, also liver-spotted, with its unsucked teats; in this posture she continues to wag her backside, like an animated floor-mop. If I then tug or caress the loose skin of her exposed neck, she almost expires with satisfaction. The only movement she is capable of is an imitative, inward flexing of her forepaws. Reduced to this state, she remains in a kind of stupor, neither awake nor asleep even after I have gone. Later I will discover her sitting or lying in her favourite position in the living room, as close as she can get to the French windows. From there she looks out for her companions, whom she knows to be barred from the house. If they do not present themselves to her for their ritual humiliation, she barks shrilly at the glass until they appear. Then she falls silent, content to have them where she wants them: at once visible and excluded.

No wonder they so often seize the opportunity, when they are out together on the Heath, to nip her on the ears and hind legs, even to send her flying head over heels. Whereupon she comes yelping to me for protection, hurls herself into my arms, and slavers in loving relief over any part of me that her tongue can reach.

Next: the beauty and aristocrat of the trio, the long-haired golden labrador. Everything about him suggests indolent grace and self-assurance. He came to me complete with an elaborate pedigree and a listing of the prizes won by his forebears at dog shows in various parts of the country.

I remember being amused by the contrast then between his diminutive stature and the amount of documentation he carried. Yet he grew to his present size and dignity soon enough. The one thing about him that has not changed since then is the colour of his coat. It was hardly "golden" when he was a puppy and is not golden now. If I had to describe it with a single adjective, I would call it beige. But what a beige! It is the colour of wheat stubble: not when the stalks have just been cut, but a few weeks later, when they have acquired a faint, silvery sheen. To the touch, however, his fur has always been as soft as cashmere. It falls in clusters of girl-like curls on his chest; more curls hang down from his legs; there are fringes of them even over his paws. Setting all this off is an amber eye and black-rimmed lips. To see how he stands, lies, sits, walks sedately, raises his head, stares about him, is to be convinced that he knows just how beautiful he is.

Handsome is as handsome does, however. The noble shape of his head and shoulders, the austere luxury of his coat, the limpidity and shapeliness of his eyes, are not the signs of a noble character. Far from it. He is mine, he knows he is mine, he incessantly craves my attention; yet when we are out on our walks he will flirt with strangers, anywhere, at any time, drawing their attention to himself, attaching himself to them – only to move away whenever they try to stroke him. Once gone, they are forgotten. He is ready immediately for the next encounter. He prefers to walk rather than run (the better to be gazed at, I suspect). A stately lope is the nearest he ever comes to hurrying, a motion that looks so easy you would think he could keep it up for ever; but he is idle as well as vain, and tires soon, and reverts to his usual saunter. Not even the scent of a bitch on heat will energize him, make him skittish, refractory, obsessively expectant in manner, as it always does to his fellow male. Naturally he resents any attention I give to either of the other two. He sulks whenever I show them affection, growling from low in his chest, letting his black-edged upper lip flicker off his canines. Later, avoiding eye contact, he will present his handsome profile to me, as if in condescension and invitation.

Finally, black and tan in colour, sleek of coat, long-legged, thin-necked, hammer-headed, there is the dobermann. Strangers do not care for him at all. Women, especially, are nervous of him. They may be eager to try to stroke the labrador, and even to encourage their children to do so, but they draw away when this one passes by – or, even more alarmingly, when he pauses to look at them, his head held high, chest exposed, black eyes shining. The hair of his coat is even shorter and more tightly packed than that of the mongrel, but only I know how smooth and supple it is, like well-worked leather. He would take off the fingers of anyone else who tried to touch him. Forever on the qui vive, snorting and shaking spittle from his jaws, his docked, thumb-shaped tail closed down over his vulnerable rearward parts, he runs like a racehorse, head moving up and down, paws springing sharply from the ground with every stride. There is something of the racehorse, too, about the angle at which his hind legs meet his body.

All unfamiliar dogs he regards as a potential threat, as enemies to be cowed and then held in contempt. He distinguishes neither between pekinese and alsatians among them; nor between adults and children among people. He is the only one of the three who has ever got into fights with other dogs on the Heath, and whom I have had to take home (and thence to the vet) with torn ears and wounded flanks. About a year ago I decided to muzzle him before we went out, and kept this up for some months. But the contraption of black thongs and brass studs I had to affix to his jaws made him look even more threatening than before, like a masked gunman or terrorist. So I took the muzzle off; since then, though he remains as excitable as ever, and as jealous of what he conceives to be my safety as well as his own, he has shown more caution in his dealings with all the other creatures he encounters on our walks.

There they are then, the three whom I take out every day, whatever the weather or season: the slavish mongrel, the narcissist, the warrior. They are my bosom companions, the sharers of my present solitude, the bearers of passions I no longer wish to feel. The only names I have ever thought of giving them are Self One, Self Two and Self Again. It makes no difference to them. Hearing my voice, all three respond at once, whatever I call them.

April 2, 1999

Easter

By John McGahern

The morning was clear. There was no wind on the lake. There was also a great stillness. When the bells rang out for Mass, the strokes trembling on the water, they had the entire Easter world to themselves. On such an Easter morning, as we were setting out for Mass, we were always shown the sun: Look how the molten globe and all the glittering rays are dancing. The whole of heaven is dancing in its joy that Christ has risen.

Jamsie opened the porch door noiselessly. He came through the house without a sound until he stood in the doorway of the large living-room where they were sitting. He was as still as if waiting under trees for returning wild fowl. He expected the discovery to be quick. There would be a cry of surprise and reproach; he would counter by accusing them of not being watchful enough. There would be welcome and laughter. When the Ruttledges continued to converse about a visit they were expecting that same afternoon, he could contain himself no longer. Such was his continual expectation of discovery that in his eavesdropping he was almost always disappointed by the innocence he came upon.

"Ye are no good!" he cried out. "I have been standing here several minutes and haven't heard a bad word said about anybody yet."

"Jamsie!" They turned to the voice with great friendliness. As he often stole silently into the house, they showed little surprise.

"You are welcome, very welcome."

"Not a bad word said about anybody", he repeated with mocking slowness as he came forward into the room.

"We never speak badly about people. It's too dangerous."

"Then you never speak, or if you do, the pair of yous are not worth listening to."

In his dark Sunday suit, white shirt, red tie, polished black shoes, the fine silver hair brushed back from the high forehead and sharp clean features, he was shining and handsome. On the lapel of the dark suit was pinned an Easter lily. An intense vividness and sweetness of nature showed in every quick expressive movement.

"Kate", he held out an enormous hand. She pretended to be afraid to trust her hand to such strength. It was a game he played regularly. For him all forms of social intercourse were merely different kinds of play.

"God hates a coward, Kate", he demanded, and she took his hand.

Not until she cried "Easy there, Jamsie", did he release his gently tightening grip with a low cry of triumph. "You are one of God's troopers, Kate. Mister Ruttledge", he bowed solemnly.

"Mister Murphy."

"No misters here", he said. "No misters in this part of the world. Nothing but broken-down gentlemen."

"There are no misters in this house either: He that is down can fear no fall."

"Why don't you go to Mass, then, if you're that low?" "What's that got to do with it?" "You'd be like everybody else round here by now if you went to Mass."

"I'd like to attend Mass. I miss going."

"What's keeping you, then?" "I don't believe."

"I don't believe", he mimicked. "None of us believes and we go. That's no bar."

"I'd feel a hypocrite. Why do you go if you don't believe?" "To look at the girls. To see the whole performance", he declared, and then started to shake with laughter. "I go to see all the other hypocrites. Kate, what do you think of all this? You've hardly said a word."

"My parents were atheists. They taught me all that is there is what you see; all that you are is what you think and appear to be."

"The way we perceive ourselves to be and how we are perceived are often different", Ruttledge said drily.

"Pay no heed to him either. He's just trying to twist and turn. Thought pissed in the bed and thought he was sweating; his wife thought otherwise. That's how it goes. You'll get on just as good as any of them, Kate."

"I thought you didn't support the men of violence", Ruttledge fastened on the Easter lily pinned to the lapel of the dark jacket.

"I support them all." He thrust out his huge hand. "They were collecting outside the church gate today. They'll be gathering soon to march from the Monument to the graveyard. I shake hands with them all. You never know who is going to come out on top." He took pruning shears from his pocket and placed them on the table. "Thanks", he said. "They were comfort. Pure Sheffield. Great steel."

"I bought them from a stall in the Enniskillen market one Thursday", Kate said. "Would you like a whiskey?" "Now you are getting down to business, Kate, but you should know by now that wilya is a very bad word."

"Why bad?" "Look at yer man." He pointed to where Ruttledge had already taken glasses and a bottle of Powers from the cupboard and was running water into a brown jug.

"I'm slow."

"You're not one bit slow, Kate. You just weren't brought up here. You nearly have to be born into a place to know what's going on and what to do."

"He wasn't brought up here."

"Not too far off, near enough to know. He wasn't at school but he met the scholars." He raised his glass. "Good health and more again tomorrow! The crowd lying below in Fenagh aren't drinking any drinks today." There was a long silence. "Did you hear the cuckoo yet?" he asked.

"No. Not yet."

"You're very slack", he said with pleasure. "I heard her three days ago, at ten past six in the alders on McGiveney's Hill, and twice yesterday."

"How come you are the first to hear the cuckoo every year?" "I'm a sleepy fox. That's the why."

In the lull, the sound of distant drumming entered the stillness of the house. After a few seconds the drumming broke off as abruptly as it began.

"They're gathering on Selton. In a while they'll march from the Monument to the graves in Fenagh. I remember the ambush as if it was yesterday", he said reflectively.

"I was planting potatoes with my father on the hill. The sods had been turned and harted. I was dropping the splits in the holes my father made. They were dusted with lime. There was nearly always a cold blast on that hill.

"We saw them coming up through the bog in single file with the guns, and sloping on up towards Selton under cover of the hedge this side of the river. They were all very young. Some of them were not much more than boys, God bless us all. They were planning to take cover in the ditches and to ambush the tender coming from Fenagh as soon as it got to the top of Selton.

"They walked straight into a trap. The Tans had got word, and a machine gun was set up. I never heard the sound before or since: a tinny sort of rat-tat-tat.

"Mulvey's red bullock got hit in the eye with one of the first rounds and staggered in circles round the field, roaring. The poor fellas didn't stand an earthly. Those that were able did their best to escape. All of them were wounded, and they tried to hide as soon as they got as far as the bog.

"They were followed down with bloodhounds. There was an officer with a revolver and twelve to fourteen men with rifles. As soon as the bloodhounds sniffed out a man, the officer blew a whistle. Then a man with a rifle would come over. There was never more than the one shot. None of them put up a fight.

"We were in full view and had only to look down. My father warned me not to be looking and to go on dropping the splits as if nothing was happening, but you couldn't but look. They could have seen us plain as well, but they never looked our way. We could have been a cow or a horse for all the notice they took.

"We ran out of splits. We stopped all the holes and scuffled the ridges, and then my father said he'd chance it to the house for a fresh bag.

"O my father was strong in those days. He thought nothing of rising at daylight, and he'd have an acre of meadow cut with the scythe before the sun was over McGiveney's Hill. I saw him walk the eighteen miles to buy a young horse at the fair in Swanlinbar, and he'd have walked the same eighteen miles home if he hadn't bought the horse. He never spoke much. He was ignorant and thick and believed in nothing but work and having his own in everything. But we never went hungry. My poor mother was like a wren or a robin flitting to his every beck and call. The likes of him wouldn't be tolerated nowadays. They'd be hammered!" He drove his fist into his enormous palm in emphasis and resentment. "They'd have every right to be hammered."

"Wasn't your mother afraid to be in the house?" "They heard the shooting and weren't sure what it was but knew better than to open the door. They could tell my father's step on the street when he came for the splits. What could they have done anyhow if it wasn't his step?" "You went on planting?" "What else could we do? If we ran or hid they might think we were spies. All the time we could hear the bawling and roaring of Mulvey's red bullock as he staggered round in circles. After a long while they headed back for Selton without ever coming near us, two men dragging a corpse between them by an arm. The men that lay wounded on Selton they didn't shoot. All were brought to Carrick in the lorry. I often think of that line of young men filing up through the bog towards Selton in the morning and the terrible changes a few short hours can bring.

"Not until we quit setting for the day and it was close to dark did we venture down into the bog. You'd swear to God nothing had happened. There wasn't even a spent shell. Then from a clump of sallies hanging out over the river we heard 'Hel-loo . . . Hel-loo . . . Hel-loo' in a half-whisper as if the caller was half-afraid to be heard."

Jamsie laughed as he tried to capture the tension in the call between the need to be heard and the fear of being heard.

"We went to run away. In the near darkness we thought it was a ghost of one of the dead men, but he had heard our voices and knew we were children. 'Hel-loo . . . Hel-loo . . . Hel-loo . . . Hel-loo.' He was calling as hard as he was able. It was Big Bernie Reynolds in the middle of the clump of sallies out in the river. His head was just above the water. He had got into the river further up and had worked his way down till he reached his depth. That's how the bloodhounds lost his trail. They also said that the coldness of the water saved him by stopping his bleeding. Somehow he wedged himself in the middle of the sallies so that he wouldn't drown if he passed out. He was very weak. My father got him out of the river by running a rope beneath his arms. We had to go and tackle the pony. For all my father's strength, it put him to the pin of his collar to get him lifted on the cart.

"We had Big Bernie for several weeks up in the loft behind the pony's harness. The priest came and the doctor. The loft is closed now. We used a ladder. I often held the lantern while Doctor Dolan changed the bandages.

"Hel-loo. Hel-loo. Hel-loo", he suddenly called out, no longer rendering the plea as a fearful call for help, but turning it into the high cry of a bird mocking us out over the depths of the bog.

"The houses on the mountain were raided, but luckily not one of the houses round Selton was touched. If they had come and looked in the loft, we were goners. Big Bernie never spoke much. I used bring him his food and drink and take and empty his pot. He hardly ever said a word. My father gave out the rosary at night, but he never answered down any of the prayers. Maybe he was afraid there could be somebody out on the street listening. As soon as he was fit to be moved, they came for him at night with a side-car.

"Then they came for poor Taylor, the Protestant, nine fields away. The Taylors were quiet and hardworking, and they kept to themselves like all the Protestants. They knew as much about the ambush as we knew.

"Taylor's wife met them when they came to the back door. She thought they were calling about a mare they had in the *Observer* that week, and pointed them to the byre where Taylor was milking. They shot him like a dog beneath the cows and said he had confessed before he was shot. We are a beautiful people, Kate. They shot him because somebody had to be made to pay, and poor Taylor was a Protestant and the nearest to hand. All the houses around were raided the next day. They searched the loft and threw down the pony's harness, but found nothing.

"Never, never, never did Big Bernie Reynolds come back once to the house to as much as say thanks, and we could have lost our lives while he was there. We never, never had as much as a word from the night they took him away on the side-car till this very day, and we are not likely to hear now unless he rises out of the ground.

"After the war he grew rich in the town. He was on every committee in the county. As he got old he used often sit outside his shop on a warm day. Do think he'd ever recognize us as we passed?" "Couldn't you have stopped and reminded him? People often forget and are glad to be reminded."

"I'd be very apt", he said scornfully. "He knew where we lived. Would you forget if you were pulled out of the river and hid and fed in a loft for weeks. We didn't mind. You wouldn't leave a cat or a dog in the river, never mind a wounded man. In the Spring, and times when it's not even Spring, I often see myself and my father planting potatoes on the hill and that line of young men coming up through the bog and think of the changes a short hour can bring. And that's life!" he called out triumphantly.

"And it's everything!" Kate said.

"I don't see queues gathering down in Fenagh trying to get out."

He was listening again intently. The drumming was constant. "They have started to march."

"Wouldn't it be more fitting if they had a talking dummy calling out Hel-loo every minute or so instead of the poor stone soldier?" "They'd not stand for that", he said.

"Wouldn't it be better than the little stone soldier looking down the hill with his gun?" "They have left the Monument", he said. "There's no way even you could get Hel-loo out of a stone."

"All you would have to do is put a long-running tape in the head that would call out every so often."

"They'd not stand for it. They'd think you were making fun of them."

"But isn't it closer to what happened?" "It wouldn't make any differ. These are serious people. They could shoot you. God, but you'd love to be behind the ditch when the tourists get out of their cars with the cameras and to see their faces when the statue says Hel-loo. It'd be nearly worth doing it just to see their faces." He laughed and drank slowly what remained in his glass. "But I'll never forget the first Hel-loo. There was a terrible gap between the Hel- and the loo. The poor fucker was afraid he'd be heard and afraid of his arse he'd not be heard. The dead can be turned into anything", he said almost in wonderment.

"Why don't we go?" Ruttledge said.

There were primroses and violets on the banks of the lane and the dark leaf of the wild strawberry, dandelion in flower, and little vetches.

"Lord bless us, not a soul in sight on this shore", Jamsie

said when they came to the lake. "There were Sundays when this shore was black with people. There were some awful poor innocent people going then. They'd believe anything and were easily pleased. Now there's nothing but the divers and the swans."

It was too early to scent the wild mint, but they could see its rough leaves crawling along the edges of the gravel. The drumming was closer. They could hear the fifes or tin whistles. Jamsie lifted his bicycle from the hedge and cycled alongside. They hurried. When they reached the main road there was nobody else waiting. A Garda squad car came slowly round the turn. A colour party followed. They wore black shoes and pants, white shirts, black ties and gloves, black berets and dark glasses. Out in front, a lone marcher bore the tricolour. In threes the others marched. They carried placards with slogans and photos of Pearse, McDermott and Sands on green, white and gold backgrounds. The effect was somehow sinister and cheap. They were all from the North. A small crowd followed the band. In the middle of the crowd quietly walked Jimmy Joe McKiernan, reputed to be head of the Provisionals, North and South, and with the power of life and death over all who marched. A second Garda squad car followed at a discreet distance.

"One thing you can say about Jimmy Joe is that he never pushes himself out in front", Jamsie said with approval as they turned away.

"They'll probably be putting up another statue to him one these years."

"In jail, out of jail, pulled in for questioning at all hours, watched night and day by the Special Branch. Since he was a boy he's been with them, and nothing much was ever happening. It must have been a pure godsend when the North blew up."

"Have any of the marchers any idea of what really happened at Selton?" "Not a clue. They're not from here and weren't born then. Jimmy Joe is the only one who knows, and he doesn't care. All he cares about is turning it around into a bigger thing. That's why they'd never stand for your shouting dummy. It's in the other direction they want to go."

"What's that?" Ruttledge asked.

"Big show. Big blow. Importance", he shouted as he climbed on the bicycle, and turned round to bow mockingly. "I never liked yous anyhow."

They could hear him laughing as he cycled off.

The sun was now high above the lake. There was still no cloud. A child could easily believe that the whole of heaven was dancing.

April 30, 1999

Science and the Arts

By M. John Harrison

Mona was in her late thirties. Two years before we mèt she had spent some months in a psychiatric hospital. By the time it became clear that the constant pain she complained about was not imaginary but the result of a botched operation, her career was ruined and her immune system had broken down. She was anorexic, subject to panic attacks and suffering from depression.

She lived for a while in Stoke Newington, where she had a short affair with a journalist, then moved to Camden, where she took courses in pain management. She enrolled at the Slade. We were introduced about a year after that, and began seeing one another every two weeks or so. She was unhappily involved with a sculptor – a dependent, manipulative man in his fifties – and I was unhappily involved with a woman who had turned to novel-writing after a career in TV drama. For a while our mutual friends had tried to matchmake us, but they weren't successful.

Mona's flat was in a quiet crescent north of Camden High Street. It comprised three rooms (one of which she used as a studio) kitchen and bathroom. The kitchen was very small. Mona didn't eat much so she lived mainly at the other end of the flat in the room which faced on to the street. There she had a computer, some bookshelves, a sofa, and, arranged so she could watch the television from it, her bed.

The bed was a small double, made up with a quilt and a stained white throw. There were two pillows, one old and very yellowed and without a pillowcase. When the pain was bad, or when she was cold, Mona would pull the quilt up to her chin and watch television from the bed while her visitor sat on the sofa. Or half-way through the evening she would get into bed like a child with all her clothes on. It was disconcerting. Even though you knew she was dressed, there was always a moment of uncertainty when she threw back the covers to get out again.

A bad day always made Mona feel as if she was on the edge of a relapse. She phoned me at seven o'clock one evening. "I don't think I've been eating", she said. The week before, she had finally managed to end her relationship with the sculptor, who had just had major surgery of his own. I went over to Camden to see if I could help. She was glad to have someone look after her for an hour or two, but careful to make it clear that though she was attracted to me, and knew I was attracted to her, she didn't want an affair with anybody at the moment.

I said I hadn't come for that. I didn't expect a return on helping someone.

She asked if she could hug me. I said yes. I was sitting on the sofa. She knelt on the floor in front of me and I put my arms around her. It felt awkward to me but it was what she wanted.

"I'm listening to your heart", she said at one point. "It's a great comfort to me."

"You should cry as much as you want to", I said.

She knelt on the floor like that for nearly an hour. To someone coming in we would have resembled one of Egon Schiele's relentlessly awkward couples, but without the sex. All I could think was how much her knees must hurt. I hadn't seen her for a month and she was even thinner than I remembered. Eventually she got up and went to bed.

As soon as I thought she was feeling better, I cooked her a meal which we ate in front of the television. I made her promise to eat more often and take things easy for a few days. When I stood up to go at half past eleven or a quarter to twelve, she said anxiously, "Are you sure you can get home at this time of night? If it's difficult you're welcome to stay." I would be all right, I told her, home was only a few stops along the Northern line. In fact I was tired out by the effort of cooking. I wanted to go back so I could think what any of this meant.

Two days later we were in a Pizza Express. She had asked me to explain the idea of "quantum memory" to her so she could incorporate it into some work she was doing for the Slade foundation course. I was just saying something like, "Light can be a wave or a particle according to what the observer expects", when she interrupted: "This is very phallic, isn't it? Here you are talking about very small things and look what I'm doing." She was rubbing her fingers up and down the candle-holder on the table between us. I didn't know what to make of that so I said: "It is, isn't it? Ha ha," then I went back to explaining the dual nature of light.

"I've written it all down", I said.

I walked her home. She went into the bathroom and changed to a pair of cotton pyjamas and a scruffy, home-made-looking grey pullover. "I took what you said to heart", she told me. "I really did. Honestly I've been eating much more." She spread a portfolio of her work on the floor so that we could look at it. There were photographs of strange tall constructions she had made using bandages, wire, scraps of paper with quotations about illness on them. She had photographs of her surgery, and of the sculptor's. She was interested in text as object. She said that she used quotes from other people because she found it hard to trust her own opinions. I said that I had got round that in the 1970s by presenting my own opinions as quotations from other people, which seemed to authorize them for me until I had enough confidence to present them as my own. Then I made a cup of tea, watched part of a television programme about risk management, and got up to go at about half past eleven.

"It's quite late", she said. "You're welcome to stay if it's too late to get home."

"The tubes run for another hour", I said.

Earlier I had signed one of my books to her. Inside it I had written, "Eat well. Get strong. Take care." It was a novel about a woman who wanted to fly but the best she could get was a cosmetic treatment that made her look like a bird. I apologized to Mona that all my books seemed to feature women who became very ill, and that this one featured a woman who became very ill after a series of operations.

This is what I had written down for her about quantum memory.

Every particle that has ever been involved with another particle somehow remembers that involvement & takes it forward into the next transaction. Everything that has ever been joined remains joined in some way. This is only at the level of very small things.

Quantum indeterminacy:

(a) If you know where a particle is, you can't know its velocity. If you know its velocity you can't know where it is.

(b) Light can be described as both a wave-form or a particle. It is not "both at the same time": it is genuinely one or the other according to what kind of machinery you use to observe it.

Quantum particles begin as a potential of the condition we call empty space. They are then "observed", or locked into place, by the rest of the universe: that is, one of their potential states is contented by local conditions and "chosen" to become real. The option the universe didn't take up, however, still continues to exist in some more informal way.

Since each of these options can be spoken of as having a "memory" of the other, and since every mechanism for human memory proposed so far – from chemical cellular memory to a more broadly distributed holographic memory – has been discounted, some scientists have toyed with the idea that memory may be stored at the quantum level in transactions like those I've described.

As science it is speculative. As a metaphor quite nice. All the rest – quantum indeterminacy, the dual nature of light and so on – is fact, as far as fact can be ascertained using contemporary experimental tools.

It was time I learned to protect women from my enthusiasms: so the ex-scriptwriter had told me, just before she ended our relationship on the grounds that a photograph of me with an old girlfriend had appeared in the pages of *Publishing News*. Women, she believed, saw men's enthusiasm as a form of bullying. She called it "male energy". I wasn't protecting Mona from my enthusiasm by sending her confused ideas about quantum physics printed in 18-point Gill Sans Condensed Bold type. Perhaps Mona thought of enthusiasm as male energy too. Perhaps that was why she had found herself giving the candle a hand job in the Pizza Express.

Mona haunted her flat wearing her shabby pullovers with very short skirts and thick tights. She was part of the clutter, an uncompleted gesture, thin as a stick but always elegant. She was so composed that I walked past her in the living room without seeing her. When I went back in she was standing by the table with one hand flat on the tabletop, staring down at a page of the newspaper, lifting it but not quite turning it.

"Hi", I said.

"Oh, hello!" She spoke as if she had forgotten there was anyone else in the flat; or as if I had rung her up after a long absence.

"I thought you were in the other room", I said.

"No", she said. "I was here all the time."

That evening we went into the West End to see *The English Patient*. Mona walked very slowly along Shaftesbury Avenue to the cinema. We got seats at the end of a row and sat leaning a little away from each other. She had taken the outer seat so that she could stand up in the aisle when she needed to. Standing up was one of the techniques she had been taught to help manage her pain. In one scene in the film a man was supposed to be having his fingers cut off. Or perhaps it was his thumbs. You didn't see anything, but there was a sudden indrawn breath from the audience. All over the cinema people were wincing in case they did see something. Mona gasped and clutched my hand. She pulled me closer to her and we sat like that for a moment or two.

"I'm not sure about that film", she said on the way out of the cinema. "Its heart's too far in the right place." I asked her what she meant.

"Oh, I don't know", she said. "I think I need a cup of tea." When we got back to her flat, I went to the kitchen to make it. While I was in there putting tea bags in the cups and doing a bit of washing up while I waited for the kettle to boil, I heard her go into the bathroom then come out again. "I'm getting into bed", she called. "It's cold in here. Aren't you cold?" I said I was OK. When I took the tea into the front room, she had the television on. We watched that and drank our tea, and then I got up to go.

"I worry about you leaving so late", Mona said. "Are you sure you can get a train this late? It would be so easy for you to stay."

"No," I said. "Honestly, the trains seem to run forever."

"You could be mugged or anything", she said.

I laughed.

She had the bedclothes up to her chin. She was just eyes.

"I want you to stay", she said.

"That's different", I said.

I took the cups away and switched the TV off. She watched me undress. Then she lifted the edge of the quilt to encourage me to get in with her.

"I thought you'd still have your clothes on", I said.

She looked up at me anxiously, holding the quilt back so I could see.

"I'm bleeding a bit", she said. "You won't mind, will you?"

September 3, 1999

The Shortlist Season

By Ali Smith

It was the turn of the century, and the turn of the season again. I had been to the bank and now I was at a loss, so I crossed the park to get to the contemporary art gallery where an exhibition which had been written up in all the papers as culturally important was still showing.

The city was blowing about that day in the dregs of a storm which was happening (or had maybe already happened) thousands of miles away across the Atlantic; in the far distance over the park a tractor was spreading fertilizer on its lawns against the damage that winter would do. I walked under the trees. Leaves, fast and hardened, scuffed against my head and grazed my face. In front of me on the path a man was collecting fallen leaves; he looked ridiculous, large for the machine he sat on which was whirring at the too-high pitch of a full domestic vacuum-cleaner as he sucked leaves up through its nozzle, and more were falling behind him, in front of me, on the paths he'd already cleared. Leaves blew round us like birds, or painted snow. When I reached the gallery I had to brush smaller leaves off my shoulders.

Outside the front door a man was talking to some younger men. The wind blew his hair the wrong way and he held it in place with one hand, waving his other hand about. The younger men's deference to him and the angle of his back, the bend of his head on his neck, all meant the man was an authority on something. Of course, it has its own inherent narrative, he was saying, but its narrative is.

Its narrative is. But I don't know what. I couldn't make out the rest, and if I'd walked any more slowly or turned to stand

and listen then the three men would have sensed me and I would have made them uneasy. Someone, a mad person maybe, or at least a slightly dangerously incalculable person (the city being full of them) would have been listening in to their private conversation in an uncalled-for way. Wind-charred now in the warm gallery foyer I pulled my sweater over my head, and it was a little irritating to me, the fact that I could so easily have seemed mad or like one of those incalculable people to them. Mostly though, I thought with my mouth full of wool, I was irritated because I wouldn't, because I won't ever know what came after that man's is, or what exactly it was he was talking about, what he meant by saying the words he did, what he knew the inside story to be.

There were leaves caught in the hood of my sweater. Something fell out. When it hit the floor it bounced quite high and made a surprisingly sharp noise for such a small thing, and I picked it up. It was a sycamore seed, its single propeller was veined like a kind of skin and made the seed surreal: a small flying hazelnut, a wing with a shrunken head attached, a fish almost all fin. But the gallery assistant behind the postcard counter was watching me with a kind of interest, so I put the seed back inside my sweater with the leaves, folded it over my arm and listened politely as he told me that entry was free, handouts about the exhibition were also free, and illustrated catalogues were £16.50.

Usually the people who work behind the counters of galleries like this one are supercilious about the people who come to see the art, but this assistant was new, still unjaded, keen. I let him tell me all of it, the price of the small postcards, the price of the larger ones and the ones with three-dimensional effects, and the fact that the posters were sold out but the re-order would be in any day. I opened a display catalogue at a photograph of two cups of coffee on a coffee table; I flicked through it, closed it and put it back on the pile of other catalogues sealed inside cellophane. The assistant was holding out a piece of paper. It was a competition leaflet with a picture of a car on it, organized, it said, in tandem with the exhibition. If I filled in my name and address, allowed a car company to put my name on a mailing list for junk mail and could say in no more than ten words why I thought modern art mattered, I might win a car. You can fill it in later, the assistant told me, and leave it here on your way out. Or you could fill it in now if you like. You could borrow my pen.

He was beginning to annoy me. He was smiling a great deal. He was acting as if he knew me. I put the leaflet in my pocket, thanked him and took a handout.

Or maybe if I had stopped to listen to those three men talking outside, I was thinking as I pushed through the swing doors to the exhibition, maybe they wouldn't have been uneasy at all, maybe they'd have been secretly pleased, because it is always nice, one way or another, to think that someone somewhere is listening. Maybe they'd have smirked self-consciously and nodded to me to join their group, made space for me. The man holding forth might even have conceded to explain. What I'm talking about is. Or: I'm referring to the manner in which the. Who knew? I went round the gallery and looked at the pictures, the sculptures and the installations.

They had been created by male twins now in their forties, who'd been born siamese but separated soon after birth. The twins and their art were very fashionable; this exhibition, it announced on a board on the wall, had placed them on the prestigious shortlist of a current art award. Broadsheet newspapers were full of authoritative lists and shortlists just now; the best films and pop songs and historical moments of the century, the best music of the year, best novel, best poetry collection, best art. Papers had been running pictures of these twins taken just after they'd been separated, and of them as they were now, beside pictures of their sculptures or paintings and stills from their videos. The odds on them winning the art award were short, something like 3/1. I walked around the rooms in the too-hot gallery; though there were several people walking and stopping like me, we were all respectful, subdued, like people generally are at a gallery, as if in a church or a bookshop. But I was sweating. Sweat was runnelling down my back; I could feel it cooling the length of my spine. I put my hand behind my neck, just under my hairline and it came away wet. I stood in the middle of the gallery and looked at the sweat on my fingers.

It was because of the change in temperature between outside and in, or the larger temperature changes that happen in the change of a season. Or maybe, I thought as I laughed at myself inside my head and wiped my hand on my shirt, the reason I was sweating was because I would never know how the man at the door had finished his sentence. I felt a little dizzy. I felt weak. I began to wonder whether I'd caught some horrible flu virus, or something worse, something with no name, which was right now multiplying itself through the inside of me. I glanced at a man who was going past me looking at the art in the wrong direction, the other way round from the way suggested by the arrows stencilled at the front door. For instance, he looked fine. He didn't seem to be sweating. He didn't even look hot. Nobody else in the room looked hot.

I stopped beside a sculpture of a coffee table with cups on it which were half-full of something rust-coloured, a folded newspaper placed next to them. The cups had what looked like perspex fixed over their tops and the newspaper's pages were stapled together with thin metal staples all the way round it. I walked on. I could feel my legs beneath me. I kept walking at the right art gallery pace; I didn't want to seem unusual to anyone. The only sound in the rooms was occasional and came from the video installations; it was an intermittent grinding noise, like teeth in the mouth of a sleeping person recorded very close-up, or something industrial. The video screens took up three walls of a darkened room; I watched for a while, but couldn't tell what it was I was looking at. On all three walls there was something red and dark and its surface shifted, shone dully; perhaps it was the massive inside of a mouth, a tongue laid flat on a palate bone. Now I could feel my mouth, cavernous, and the way my jaw raised its bone up and became the bottom row of my teeth. I came out of the dark. I concentrated on the paintings instead.

They were uniformly huge and square, each reaching from the skirting board up to the edge of the ceiling and each pair filling a wall as if this gallery, designed at the turn of the last century, had been planned especially to fit these paintings. They were all in pairs. The first of the pairs was of something recognizable and domestic, say a teapot or a dog. The second was a near-empty canvas, cleanish, always smudged at the centre like the painter had touched it there by chance with a hand not clean enough. The images together would be titled: Teapot, 1 & 2 or: Dog, 1 & 2.

I got it. It didn't exactly take long to get. It was all about alienation and distance, wasn't it? I had only had to walk once round the gallery, which is pretty small, to get it, but I walked round a couple more times just to prove to myself that in this sweating state I could. After the third time I stopped and sat breathing on a stool in the corner, the kind that the art gallery attendants usually sit on.

The two paintings opposite me now were called Road, 1 & 2. The one on the left was of an empty tarmac road leading into middle distance with plain grass verges on either side of it. The one on the right was another canvas left almost completely empty behind its glass, just the clay-coloured smudges at its centre resembling grime or a mistaken touch. On the front of the free handout it told me that the twins liked to paint two identical works then slowly, painstakingly, to remove all paint from one of the paired canvases except for a scant trace at the centre of the gone image, and as soon as I read this I remembered I'd already known that this was what the twins did, that I had read about this process in a Sunday newspaper or somewhere similar.

I felt shopsoiled, cheated on by my own memory. I sat back on the stool, leaned my weight into the wall behind me and closed my eyes. Then I remembered: the last time I had visited an art exhibition, several months back, I had also felt so unwell that I had had to sit down. It had been at a bigger, grander gallery in the middle of the city. At the very top of the building, up several flights of stairs and along a corridor lined in marble so glassy you could see yourself reflected from the feet up as you walked along it, there were three rooms filled with the small, relentless, brightly coloured pictures a young Jewish painter had used to record the various stories of her life and her family's lives in Berlin in the 1930s and 40s before her death, inevitable, pregnant and statistical. That day, I recalled now, I had been able to look closely at only three of the hundreds of her paintings before feeling the floor under my feet start to shift and creak like the whole of the gallery beneath us – beneath all these people wandering round the rooms and listening to the story of the paintings on the hired gallery CD machines hung at their waists, the CDs whirring in small circles unimaginable to anyone when the pictures were painted – was a ship in a pitching ocean and us in its crow's nest swaying and dipping.

I had rocked in one place on my heels and toes to keep myself upright, my face uninterested, my insides terrified, until someone, a lady, pushed herself up off the padded seat in the middle of the floor, and her getting up made room for me. Then I had sat in the same room and counted the strips of wood in the floor, examining the varnished dust and stuff trapped in the spaces between them, the paintings still there, raucous colour hovering above my eye-line, until the bell for closing rang and a man in uniform came round telling everybody to leave, and I could go.

Perhaps it was art that made me sweat. Perhaps sculptures and pictures were inherently bad for me. I suppressed a laugh. It was funny. Earlier that morning I had been to the bank which gave me my mortgage; for some reason the woman behind the counter there is always telling me stories of infirmities and deaths. She is always having inconclusive tests, usually for something frightening. Perhaps, I thought to myself, I could have tests for art intolerance, like patch tests. We have the results, the doctor would say. You are sensitive to dust-mites, the hairs of cats and horses, shellfish, metals related to nickel, and several forms of cultural expression. I would breathe a sigh of relief. I would discover, not too late, that my life could have been symptom-free and simple all along, a matter of deep, healthy, fluid-free breaths if only I'd known to not go near art. After that I would visit theatres and galleries and cinemas and bookshops drowsily, in the haze of antihistamines, my senses so blunt that I wouldn't care in the slightest what the inherent narrative was or might be.

I always seem to get that woman serving me at the bank. Canadian, dark and thin, she has frail unsunned skin; her face through the saliva-specked double-reinforced glass is always pale. That morning, before I had felt so suddenly at a loss and had decided to take the day off work and spend some time at the contemporary art gallery, she told me a sad story while she added up my cheques. A bank colleague, only thirty-three, in fact only thirty-three last week. Year and a half ago a lump in her arm size of a small satsuma. Size of a clementine. Operated on. Given all-clear. Six weeks ago terrible headaches. Went back to hospital. Riddled all through. Died yesterday. Only thirty-three. Imagine. Divorced. Daughter aged four who had said to another bank colleague called Mary who was visiting, Mummy is in the hospital and might not be coming back.

I nodded from the other side, said things, signed the pay-ing-in slip, put it in the hollow space banks have for passing things through. My heart had grown bulky inside me one more time; one more time I was resolving behind my sympa-thetic face to change my branch. The woman was pressing something up against the inside glass layer at me, a grainy photograph, faxed or photocopied, of some people smiling at a party or in a pub. That's the woman who died on the right, she was saying; did I recognize her? The faces were inky and shadowed and the picture bleeding to white in the several folds and creases in the copy; it had been through many hands. So do something frivolous, the woman had shouted after me through the glass as I left the bank. Be sure and do something frivolous today.

Something frivolous: I had gone to an art gallery. I was sweating. I was sitting on a stool in an art gallery with my eyes shut.

I opened them and I saw a small girl of perhaps three or four smiling at me. When I smiled back, she stopped smiling and hid round the back of the legs of her mother who was standing in the middle of the room talking in a polite hush to another woman. The child swung round her mother's legs, pinning them both with her arms. She let go. She flung herself into the middle of the floor. She jumped from square to square of stone. She ignored Road 2 and stood in front of Road 1. Launching herself at the road as if she were about to run down it, she hit the picture, flat, with the weight of her whole body. The picture shuddered on the wall. The child made an amazed noise. She stood back and touched her nose.

Ow, she said.

Oh god, the mother said. Oh god, Sophie. Oh.

She turned to me. I'm so sorry, she said. I'm sorry. She just. Sorry.

No, I said, I'm not the. I mean. I'm –

I stood up. Now the mother was rubbing with a tissue at the two clear prints her daughter's hands had made on the glass. She was laughing, embarrassed, swearing under her breath. Sophie, she said.

No, I said. Don't – Please don't touch the paintings.

Oh, the woman said. Right. I'm sorry.

She stepped back, stood holding the tissue in the air, not knowing what to do.

She put it in her bag. She turned, pretty and flustered, and exchanged a glance with her friend who was holding the child by the shoulders and smiling, eyes lowered not to laugh, looking down at the top of the child's head. The child was singing something impenetrable, doing a dance again.

It's okay, I said. It's just that we can't, you know, have anyone touching the paintings.

I'm really sorry, the woman said again. Come on, Sophie, we've got to go now.

Both women made to gather the child into an anorak.

No, you can remain in the gallery, I said. It's fine. But just, well. Just don't let it happen again.

The woman relaxed. She was thanking me. But a real attendant was coming over, so I smiled what I imagined was a stern, official, goodbye kind of smile to the women, and turned to go. So that they wouldn't realize, I stopped the attendant as he passed and asked him quietly when the gallery closed. The women behind me with the child would think he was giving me orders about work, or perhaps that I was giving them to him.

The attendant looked at me with the eyes and the hauteur of someone who knows everything there is to know. But it was all right. He didn't know anything. The gallery closes at six tonight, he said.

Thanks, I said. And when does the exhibition finish?

This exhibition closes on the thirtieth, he said.

I strolled through the room whose walls could have been the insides of someone's mouth, and out the other side. I pulled my sweater on over my head. I didn't care. I was feeling better. I would go for a walk. I would throw myself into the day. I was inspired, I was calm; calm as good suburban turf and every bit as green I would saunter across the Thames swinging my arms, the water swirling and sucking beneath me and the policemen down in the drowning-station arguing with each other over their mugs of sweetened tea.

As I left the gallery I heard someone calling behind me. Maybe I'd been found out. Someone was running and it was after me; as he neared I could hear he was quite short of breath. It was the assistant who had told me what was free and what wasn't when I'd first gone in. Maybe he wanted my leaflet back, completed, with the ten-word-phrase on it, modern art is important to me because. I tried quickly to think something up.

He ran strangely, his hand clenched out before him. Wait, he called as he ran. Wait. You dropped these. They fell out. I saw them.

He looked desperate and pleased, filled with terrible import, like a messenger bringing good news about a medieval battle in a play or a film. I felt in my pocket for my wallet, but it was there. I wondered what else it was I could have dropped. I looked to see.

His hand was full of broken leaves and seeds with unlikely wings.

October 15, 1999

A Beautiful Restoration

By Dilys Rose

Before the Nazis and the Communists, pani Anna says, this place was a palace.

I nod and go on with my work. My boss is not really talking to me about the hotel, she's just thinking aloud. Though the exterior of the building is soot-black, it is still beautiful but the interior has suffered and, for pani Anna, restoration has become something of an obsession. She has spent so many thousand zloty on restoration – the cost of wallpaper alone would have been enough for me to buy a small apartment – and renovation too. The bedrooms are modern and comfortable – I know people like the rooms, especially foreigners. If I meet them in the corridor as they're going out to find breakfast and I'm off home to sleep after a night shift, they smile and say hello. In the place I was before, which hasn't changed at all since independence, I was only ever greeted by grunts and groans.

I like the night. I can get on with my work without too many interruptions and when I'm done, there's no need to pretend to be busy. Mostly it's ironing, folding and stacking linen and filling up the trolleys with soap, bottled water, shower gel and shampoo, toilet rolls and bin bags. Tonight I also have a frilly shirt to wash, buckled boots to polish. I make extra money from washing. Good enough money. There's always the chance that a light bulb might explode, the batteries of a TV remote run down, a toilet become blocked. On night shift I don't like guddling around with toilets while the guests, in their night clothes, stand over me and get in the way, or sprawl on the beds and behave as if I'm not there.

Worse can happen. There's illness – for some reason guests need a doctor much more often at night than during the day when it's a lot easier to get hold of one. During the small hours I've witnessed a birth and two deaths; one simply from drink, one from drink and sex and heart failure combined. Drink causes a lot of trouble and mess, spilled or broken bottles, blood and vomit on the carpet, the bed, the wallpaper. Mess and fights. I deal with the mess but for fights I call Dmitri, the night porter. He's big and strong and doesn't waste time, just barges in. If the door is bolted on the inside, Dmitri presses his bony forehead against the door and says: You have one minute, starting from now, before I break in. So far, Dmitri's threat has always worked, which is just as well. Pani Anna wouldn't be too happy about a broken door. In fact, I think Dmitri would be more likely to lose his job over a broken door than a smashed nose. And visitors: I see the girls in their narrow heels and split skirts flitting down the corridors like moths. I see them sneaked into the lifts and, later, hustled down the back stairs and out into the night. I see the rooms the next morning. The girls are better fed these days and probably own prettier underwear now that there's more than black market goods to choose from. Pani Anna knows this kind of thing goes on but as long as guests and visitors are discreet, it means nothing to her. For Housekeeping it means extra work – more linen and towels to be changed, more airing of rooms and scrubbing stains off the new, soft carpets.

Pani Anna cares a lot about carpets, wallpaper, about furnishings, and dreams of restoring downstairs to exactly how it was before the Nazis and the Communists: marble columns, gleaming wood panelling, flashing chandeliers and heavy damask drapes. The work is a long way from finished and she worries constantly about running out of money. The new government has given her some financial help – the hotel is an important historic building – but not enough.

Not nearly enough, says pani Anna, with the costs of materials and labour rising every day. And just look at the news: deficit may sink zloty. Where will we all be then?

The zloty is not a ship. How can it sink, or float? All I know is that I need every shift to make ends meet.

Pani Anna has a friend in Germany, a man who makes money from money. He has promised – for what reason she hasn't said, though Dmitri and I have our ideas – not to let her plans for a beautiful restoration collapse into tragedy or farce. But often, after a phone call, pani Anna is angry or gloomy, or both. She sits at reception, rests her pale, round elbows on the newly varnished horseshoe desk and drinks scotch and soda. She won't touch Polish vodka and don't even mention Russian! A good-looking woman, though the whisky and the worry are making her grey and puffy around the eyes. She should go out more, sit in the sun. Summer will not last forever.

Of course the hotel has always had more interesting guests than drunken, whoring businessmen. Its fame comes not only from its frozen music, as pani Anna calls the architecture of the building. These are not her own words; they belong to somebody famous, I don't know who. The hotel has been host to many famous people. It was here that, in 1948 – the year I was born – an International Congress was held. Writers and artists, film stars and philosophers gathered in this very building to discuss what to do about our poor, devastated country. People say pan Picasso first drew his famous fat dove of peace here, in this very building.

At that time, the interior was in a very bad condition, smashed windows and furniture, charred walls. There was a paper shortage too – well, there was a shortage of almost everything. People say that pan Picasso first drew the dove on his bedroom wall. The register from the congress disappeared – some say it was confiscated by the secret police, others that it went up in flames but anyway, it's gone, so nobody knows who slept where. Maybe the story of the dove on the wall is just a legend. A place like this has many legends, one on top of the other.

Now after a long absence, we have international visitors

again, for the festival. During the day, music spills from the bedrooms, bright and clear as mineral water, vodka. From room seventy-seven I've been hearing heavenly singing. The voice belongs to a young Italian who even after being up very late – I know how late! – will stop in the corridor, sweep back his hair, put a hand on his heart and bow. This is an act: I know he is practising and I am a substitute for his audience but still I blush and simper and scurry off to my housekeeper's room as if I'm very busy, as if I've just remembered some urgent task. Really, I'm embarrassed and ashamed of my dry, colourless hair, my cheap shoes.

Dmitri says he's a gay. He says this because the singer – whose name, I think, should be Angelo but is Giuseppe – doesn't sing in his deep speaking voice but as high as a woman, as a soprano.

– Sounds like a castrati, Dmitri says. And the costume! Have you seen his costume? High-heeled boots, frilly blouse. A gay. Crime against nature, he says, pleased with himself and his certainty.

God, everybody knows this country has seen real crimes against nature – and not just seen them. I don't argue with him. On the night shift, I have no one else to call on and sometimes I really need big, bison-headed Dmitri to help me out.

And yes, I've seen the singer's clothes. I have some of them with me at this moment; the shirt with the lace cuffs, the high boots with the silver buckles. He called me to his room, around one. He had changed out of his costume into jeans and a white T-shirt. His chin was blue with stubble and his arms were covered with thick, dark hair, like fur. He is not tall and his nose is too big to call his face perfect but what does perfect mean but a set of rules? He was tired and a little tipsy – not drunk, not like the stringless puppets you can see on every street corner – but bright-eyed, lit up. His bedside table was strewn with bouquets of flowers, still in their cellophane.

– Please, one moment, I said, and rushed out of the room. All I had in my supplies cupboard was an ugly ceramic jug, not nearly big enough and with a crazy slogan on the side: The Flowering State. That jug would not do. I phoned reception.

– Dmitri. Bring vases, blue ones. Two or three.

– Blue ones are only for reception.

– Blue vases, Dmitri. Please. And please hurry.

Dmitri never does anything quickly. I went out into the corridor and paced about in front of the lift. How slow Dmitri was! I should have fetched the vases myself. The flowers would be in water already, the singer would be bending his head, his hair falling into his eyes, burying his face in the blooms, turning his big nose from side to side, breathing in the perfume . . . . Dmitri's head appeared in the glass window of the lift. The door creaked open and he stepped out, a blue glass vase wedged in the crook of each arm, his broad faced pressed between them. Good vases he'd brought me, with heavy, swirly bases. Hard to knock over.

– Who puts flowers in water at this time of night?

– The Italian, I said. Thanks. Have to go.

Dmitri noisily sucked air through his crowded teeth, then clumped back into the lift, slowly shaking his head.

By the time I reached the singer's door I was out of breath and, I expect, red in the face. It's still so hot, even at night, though the leaves on the trees have turned gold and begun to fall. I knocked on the door with my elbow. When Giuseppe opened it and saw me standing there, half-hidden by blue glass, he gave me such a smile that I thought I would drop the vases and break them as well as my toes but then . . . then he took my face in his cool hands and – I still don't quite believe it – kissed me on both cheeks and ushered me into his room.

Giuseppe, the angel Giuseppe filled the vases with water and asked me to help him arrange the flowers, one vase each. This is not normally part of my duties but who would refuse such a sweet-smelling task? It was more of an honour than a chore to sit at the oval, glass-topped table, selecting stems from the bouquets spread in front of me. Roses, lilies, chrysanthemums; the perfume rising from the table, curling around us, drifting into our nostrils, mouths, our hair. The angel Guiseppe didn't squeeze the stems the way Dmitri does when pani Anna asks him to arrange displays for reception, he balanced them on an open palm and used his fingertips to guide them into position. Stems matter. Stems are like arteries. I've told Dmitri this but he continues to clamp them in his big fist. So, I suppose, he doesn't look like a gay.

While we were filling the vases the angel Giuseppe spoke to me, in Italian. I know the sound of the language because, on night shift, I sometimes listen to opera on the radio: it makes a change from the American pop music people can't get enough of these days. I couldn't understand a word but I could hear the angel's voice squeaking and grating, his throat hurting.

– Too much singing, he said, pointing to his open mouth. His lips were red from wine, teeth white: no gaps, no twisted stumps. His tongue, I could see his tongue, pink and curling. My ears burned; I was blushing again. I slipped the first few stems into the vase and stood up.

– Excuse me, something else you want? I said, in my horrible English. I know my English is horrible but Italian for me is no more than a wish, a dream.

– Yes yes, I forget . . .

He stood up, praising my flower arrangement over his own, went into the bathroom and came out with his boots and shirt.

– Please, can you clean, for tomorrow?

– Of course, of course. No problem. Thank you, please, I said, nodding and backing out of the room like the grovelling servant in too many bad films.

Earlier tonight, before the singer distracted me, I was ironing pillowcases and looking up from those endless bleached squares at the old, stained wallpaper which was jumping with red and green dots after all that white linen. I was thinking about pan Picasso and his fat dove, and wondering how many times the walls had been papered since the year of my birth.

In my housekeeper's room, the door is locked and I'm alone with my magazines, my kettle and tea bags, the stacks of ironed linen and towels. The linen is, of course, white, the towels too. There are plenty of good enough red (now pink) ones from before independence but pani Anna won't have them used unless a guest disgraces him- or herself. (I don't think many guests understand pani Anna's towel code.) Nearly always, it's a man who slips up, or a man and woman together but I try to be open-minded, not to discriminate.

There has been – and sadly still is, too much discrimination. Already, in the newly restored old town, over fresh, cheerful paint in colours we haven't seen for decades, the spray can and stencil graffiti are again making their ugly, hateful marks. After living with grey crumbling buildings for so long, with broken windows, broken promises and captive spirits, could we not, for a short while, enjoy the fresh paint, the calm sheen of unsmashed glass? It's a small improvement, not important, I know, but this country has seen so much destruction. Too much, too many lives crushed by one set of rules or another, this country which has the shape of a jellyfish – out and in, here and there, stretch and squeeze – a strong, stubborn jellyfish all the same, one which refuses to die no matter how many times it's stamped on. But what must it be like to live in a country with fixed, definite outlines, borders which haven't strayed for centuries, like Italy, say, its shapely high-heeled boot dipping its toe in the Mediterranean?

Carefully I put down the angel Giuseppe's boots, so as not to mark the leather which is soft and supple and smells like money. It does, it really does smell like banknotes – or else banknotes smell like good Italian leather. I pick up the shirt; such fine cotton, it's almost transparent, weighs nothing. I press it to my face and breathe in sweat and cologne; olives, sun, salt. I breathe in and in until my head spins and I have to sit down on the old battered chair in which I've passed many quiet night hours.

Most of the guests will be asleep by now. Dmitri will be dozing at reception, hoping that none of the stragglers falling in from the casinos will want room service – vodka, beer, champagne, cheese, ham, caviar. The angel Giuseppe will be lying on his big bed, naked I expect, naked I'm sure, in this heat, on his back or his side, his head resting on the pillowslip I ironed last night. How differently I'd have ironed the linen, had I imagined this: I'd have pressed it smooth with the flat of my hand, the weight of my body.

It's quiet now, except for the generator from which there is no escape. Even if I doze off in my chair I can hear its eternal grumble. No silence here, even in sleep. I fill the sink. The water mustn't be too hot, only warm, and the soap mild. I test the temperature with my elbow. Too hot. I leave it to cool down. In time it will reach the ideal temperature – blood heat. The room, too, is hot, airless, a tatty box. I toss my cardigan on the chair. No need to be tidy. Nobody ever comes here. Soon I'll wash the shirt, polish the boots . . . .

Taking off my cardigan wasn't enough; it felt like another half-measure, another compromise and now that all my clothes are on the chair it's easy to pull the shirt over my head, slip my rough, blunt fingers through the lace cuffs and let the fine white cotton slide down and cover my nakedness, cover but not obscure the neglected architecture of my body, its frozen music, as pani Anna would say.

The boots stand beneath my ironing board, a little dusty, of course, you can't have restoration without dust . . . the boots too. Only a little too big. Not heavy at all and cool against my hot legs. I unpin my hair, let it fall around my shoulders. It doesn't exactly swing when I turn my head, it doesn't fall over my face like a curtain when I place a hand on my heart and bow. No sound comes when I open my mouth but here, in my ugly little room, dressed in the angel Giuseppe's shirt and boots, it occurs to me that this could once have been a bedroom. Anybody might have slept in it, even pan Picasso.

With the spatula I use to shift stubborn clots of mud from

the shower cubicles, I pick loose a corner of wallpaper and begin to scrape. The strip peels off quite easily at first, right down to the yellow plaster. Then it becomes stubborn and clings to the wall. In the top corner of the plaster, a faint curving line swings between two raw edges of paper. I go back to where I started from and loosen the next strip. It, too, curls away from the wall. The curving line continues across the newly-bared patch of wall. Above it, I can now see a small black dot. I keep scraping. With the angel's voice in my head, the memory of his mouth on my cheeks, I too become part of a beautiful restoration.

December 24, 1999

Lone Pine

By David Malouf

Driving at speed along the narrow dirt highway, Harry Picton could have given no good reason for stopping where he did. There was a pine. Perhaps it was that – its deeper green and conical form among the scrub a reminder out here of the shapeliness and order of gardens, though this particular pine was of the native variety.

May was sleeping. For the past hour, held upright by her seatbelt, she had been nodding off and waking, then nodding off again like a comfortable baby.

Harry was used to having her doze beside him. He liked to read at night, May did not. It made the car, which was heavy to handle because of the swaying behind of the caravan, as familiar almost as their double bed.

Driving up here was dreamlike. As the miles of empty country fell away with nothing to catch the eye, no other vehicle or sign of habitation, your head lightened and cleared itself – of thoughts, of images, of every wish or need. Clouds filled the windscreen. You floated.

The clouds up here were unreal. They swirled up so densely and towered to such an infinite and unmoving height that driving, even at a hundred Ks an hour, was like crawling along at the bottom of a tank.

A flash of grey and pink flared up out of a dip in the road. Harry jerked the wheel. Galahs! They might have escaped from a dozen backyard cages, but were common up here. They were after water. There must have been real water back there that he had taken for the usual mirage. Like reflections of the sky, which was pearly at this hour and flushed with coral, they clattered upwards and went streaming away behind.

"May", he called. But before she was properly awake they were gone. "Sorry, love", she muttered. "Was it something good?" Still half-asleep, she reached into the glovebox for a packet of lollies, unwrapped one, passed it to him, then unwrapped another and popped it into her mouth. Almost immediately she was dozing again with the lolly in her jaw, its cherry colour seeping through into her dreams.

They were on a trip, the first real trip they had ever taken, the trip of their lives.

Back in Hawthorn they had a paper run. Seven days a week and twice on weekdays, Harry tossed the news over people's fences on to the clipped front lawns: gun battles in distant suburbs, raids on marijuana plantations, bank holdups, traffic accidents, baby bashings, the love lives of the stars.

He knew the neighbourhood – he had to: how to get around it by the quickest possible route. He had got that down to a fine art. Conquest of Space, it was called, just as covering it all twelve times a week in an hour and a quarter flat was the Fight against Time. He had reckoned it up once. In twenty-seven years bar a few months he had made his round on ten thousand seven hundred occasions in twelve thousand man-hours, and done a distance of a hundred thousand miles. That is, ten times round Australia. Those were the figures.

But doing it that way, piecemeal, twice a day, gave you no idea of what the country really was: the distances, the darkness, the changes as you slipped across unmarked borders.

Birds that were exotic down south, like those galahs, were everywhere up here, starting up out of every tree. The highways were a way of life with their own population: hitch-hikers, truckies, itinerant fruit-pickers and other seasonal workers of no fixed address, bikies loaded up behind and wearing space helmets, families with all their belongings packed into a station wagon and a little girl in the back waving or sticking out her tongue, or a boy putting up two fingers in the shape of a gun and mouthing Bang, Bang, You're Dead, kids in panel-vans with a couple of surf-boards on the rack chasing the ultimate wave. Whole tribes that for one reason or another had never settled. Citizens of a city the size of Hobart or Newcastle that was always on the move. For three months (that was the plan), he and May had come out to join them.

Back in Hawthorn a young fellow and his wife were giving the paper run a go.

For five weeks now, their home in Ballard Crescent had been locked up, empty, ghosting their presence with a lighting system installed by the best security firm in the state that turned the lights on in the kitchen, just as May did, regular as clockwork, at half-past five; then, an hour later, lit the lamp in their living-room and flicked on the TV; then turned the downstairs lights off again at nine and a minute later lit the reading lamp (just the one) on Harry's side of the bed in the front bedroom upstairs.

Harry had spent a good while working out this pattern and had been surprised at how predictable their life was, what narrow limits they moved in. It hadn't seemed narrow. Now, recalling the smooth quilt of their bed and the reading lamp being turned on, then off again, by ghostly hands, he chuckled. It'd be more difficult to keep track of their movements up here.

There was no fixed programme – they took things as they came. They were explorers, each day pushing on into unknown country. No place existed till they reached it and decided to stop.

"Here we are, mother", Harry would say, "home sweet home. How does it look?" – and since it was seldom a place that was named on the map they invented their own names according to whatever little event or accident occurred that made it memorable – Out-of-Nescaf Creek, Lost Tin-opener, One Blanket Plains – and before they drove off again Harry would mark the place on their road map with a cross.

This particular spot, as it rose out of the dusk, had already named itself.

Lone Pine it would be, unless something unexpected occurred.

"Wake up, mother", he said as the engine cut. "We're there."

Two hours later they were sitting over the remains of their meal. The petrol lamp hissed, casting its light into the surrounding dark. A few moths barged and dithered. An animal, attracted by the light or the unaccustomed scent, had crept up to the edge of a difference they made in the immemorial tick and throb of things, and could be heard just yards off in the grass. No need to worry. There were no predators out here.

Harry was looking forward to his book. To transporting himself, for the umpteenth time, to Todgers, in the company of Cherry and Merry and Mr Pecksniff, and the abominable Jonas – he had educated himself out of Dickens.

May, busily scrubbing their plates in a minimum of water, was as usual telling something. He did not listen.

He had learned over the years to finish the Quick Crossword while half tuned in to her running talk, or to do his orders without making a single blue. It was like having the wireless on, a comfortable noise that brought you bits and pieces of news. In May's case, mostly of women's complaints. She knew an inordinate number of women who had found lumps in their breast and gone under the knife, or lost kiddies, or had their husbands go off with younger women.

For some reason she felt impelled to lay at his feet these victims of life's grim injustice, or of men's unpredictable cruelty, as if, for all his mildness, he too were one of the guilty. As, in her new vision of things, he was. They all were.

Three years ago she had discovered, or rediscovered, the church – not her old one, but a church of a newer and more personal sort – and had been trying ever since to bring Harry in.

She gave him her own version of confessions she had heard people make of the most amazing sins and of miraculous conversions and cures. She grieved over the prospect of their having, on the last day, to go different ways, the sheep's path or the goat's. She evoked in terms that distressed him a Lord Jesus who seemed to stand on pretty much the same terms in her life as their cats, Peach and Snowy, or her friends from the Temple, Eadie and Mrs McVie, except that she saw Him, Harry felt, as a secret child now grown to difficult manhood that she had never told him about and who sat between them, invisible but demanding, at every meal.

Harry, who would have defended her garrulous piety against all comers, regarded it himself as a blessed shame. She was a good woman spoiled.

Now, when she started up again, he vanished into himself, and while she chattered on in the background, slipped quietly away. Down the back steps to his veggies, to be on his own for a bit. To feel in his hands the special crumbliness and moisture of the soil down there and watch, as at a show, the antics of the lighting system in their empty house, ghosting their lives to fool burglars who might not be fooled.

Harry woke. His years on the paper run had made him a light sleeper. But with no traffic sounds to give the clue, no night-trains passing, you lost track. When he looked at his watch it was just eleven.

He got up, meaning to slip outside and take a leak. But when he set his hand to the doorknob, with the uncanniness of a dream-happening, it turned of its own accord.

The young fellow who stood on the step was as startled as Harry was.

In all that emptiness, with not a house for a hundred miles in any direction and in the dead of night, they had come at the same moment to opposite sides of the caravan door: Harry from sleep, this youth in the open shirt from – but Harry couldn't imagine where he had sprung from. They faced one another like sleepers whose dreams had crossed, and the youth, to cover his amazement, said "Hi" and gave a nervous giggle.

He was blond, with the beginnings of a beard. Below him in the dark was a woman with a baby. She was rocking it in a way that struck Harry as odd. She looked impatient. At her side was a boy of ten or so, sucking his thumb.

"What is it?" Harry asked, keeping his voice low so as not to wake May. "Are you lost?" He had barely formulated the question, which was meant to fit this midnight occasion to a world that was normal, a late call by neighbours who were in trouble, when the young man showed his hand. It held a gun.

Still not convinced of the absolute reality of what was happening, Harry stepped back into the narrow space between their stove and the dwarf refrigerator, and in a moment they were all in there with him – the youth, the woman with the baby, the boy, whose loud-mouthed breathing was the only sound among them.

Harry's chief concern still was that they should not wake May.

The gunman was a good-looking young fellow of maybe twenty. He wore boardshorts and a shirt with pineapples on a background that had once been red but showed threads now of a paler colour from too much washing. He was barefoot, but so scrubbed and clean that you could smell the soap on him under the fresh sweat.

He was sweating. The woman was older. She too was barefoot, but what you thought in her case was that she lacked shoes.

As for the ten-year-old, with his heavy lids and open-mouthed, asthmatic breathing, they must simply have found him somewhere along the way. He resembled neither one of them and looked as if he had fallen straight off the moon. He clung to the woman's skirt, and was, Harry decided, either dog-tired or some sort of dill. He had his thumb in his mouth and his eyelids fluttered as if he was about to fall asleep on his feet.

"Hey", the youth said, suddenly alert.

Down at the sleeping end, all pink and nylon-soft in her ruffles, May had sat bolt upright.

"Harry", she said accusingly, "what are you doing? Who are those people?"

"It's all right, love", he told her.

"Harry", she said again, only louder.

The youth gave his nervous giggle. "All right", he said, "you can get outa there." Not yet clear about the situation, May looked at Harry.

"Do as he says", Harry told her mildly.

Still tender from sleep, she began to grope for her glasses, and he felt a wave of odd affection for her. She had been preparing to give this young fellow a serve.

"You can leave those", the youth told her. "I said leave 'em! Are you deaf or what?" She saw the gun then, and foggily, behind this brutal boy in the red shirt, the others, the woman with the baby.

"Harry", she said breathlessly, "who are these people?" He took a step towards her. It was, he knew, her inability to see properly that most unnerved her. Looking past the man, which was a way also of denying the presence of the gun, she addressed the shadowy woman, but her voice had an edge to it. "What is it?" she asked. "Is your baby sick?" The woman ignored her. Rocking the baby a little, she turned away and told the youth fiercely: "Get it over with, will ya? Get 'em outa here." May, who had spoken as woman to woman, was deeply offended. But the woman's speaking up at last gave life to the boy.

"I'm hungry", he whined into her skirt. "Mummy? I'm hungreee!" His eye had caught the bowl of fruit on their fold-up table. "I wanna banana!"

"Shuddup, Dale", the woman told him, and put her elbow into his head.

"You can have a banana, dear", May told him.

She turned to the one with the gun.

"Can he have a banana?" The child looked up quickly, then grabbed.

"Say ta to the nice lady, Dale", said the youth, in a voice rich with mockery.

But the boy, who really was simple-minded, lowered the banana, gaped a moment, and said sweetly: "Thank you very much." The youth laughed outright.

"Now", he said, and there was no more humour, "get over here." He made way for them and they passed him while the woman and the boy, who was occupied with the peeling of his banana, passed behind. So now it was May and Harry who were squeezed in at the entrance end.

"Right" the youth said. "Now –". He was working up the energy in himself. He seemed afraid it might lapse. "The car keys. Where are they?" Harry felt a rush of hot anger.

Look, feller, he wanted to protest, I paid thirty-three thousand bucks for that car. You just fuck off. But May's hand touched his elbow, and instead he made a gesture towards the fruit bowl where the keys sat – now, why do we keep them there? – among the apples and oranges.

"Get 'em, Lou." The woman hitched the baby over her shoulder so that it stirred and burbled, and was just about to reach for the keys when she saw what the boy was up to and let out a cry. "Hey you, Dale, leave that, you little bugger. I said leave it!" She made a swipe at him, but the boy, who was more agile than he looked, ducked away under the youth's arm, crowing and waving a magazine.

"Fuck you, Dale", the woman shouted after him.

In her plunge to cut him off she had woken the baby, which now began to squall, filling the constricted space of the caravan with screams.

"Shut it up, willya?" the youth told her. "And you, Dale, belt up, or I'll clip y' one. Gimme that." He made a grab for the magazine, but the boy held on. "I said, give it to me!"

"No, Kenny, no, it's mine. I found it."

They struggled, the man cursing, and at last he wrenched

it away. The boy yowled, saying over and over with a deep sense of grievance: "It's not fair, it's not fair, Kenny. I'm ·the one that found it. It's mine."

Harry was flooded with shame. The youth, using the gun, was turning the pages of the thing.

"Someone left it in a café", Harry explained weakly. "Under a seat." The youth was incensed. He blazed with indignation. "See this, Lou? See what the kid found?"

But the woman gave him only the briefest glance. She was preoccupied with the baby. Moving back and forth in the space between the bunks, she was rocking the child and sweet-talking it in the wordless, universal dialect, somewhere between syllabic spell-weaving and an archaic drone, that women fall into on such occasions and which sets them impressively apart. The others were hushed.

May, lowering her voice to a whisper, said: "Look here, if you're in some sort of trouble – I mean" – She indicated the gun. "There's no need of that."

But the youth had a second weapon now. "You shut up", he told her fiercely.

"Just you shut up. You're the ones who've got trouble. What about this, then?" and he shook the magazine at her.

She looked briefly, then away. She understood the youth's outrage because she shared it. When he held the thing out to her she shook her head, but he was implacable.

"I said, look!" he hissed.

Because of the woman's trouble with the baby he had lowered his voice again, but the savagery of it was terrible. He brandished the thing in her face and Harry groaned.

"Is this the sort of thing you people are into?" But the ten-year-old, excited now beyond all fear of chastisement, could no longer contain himself.

"I seen it", he crowed.

"Shuddup, Dale."

"I seen it . . ."

"I'll knock the bloody daylights out of you if you don't belt up!"

"A cunt, it's a cunt. Cunt, cunt, cunt!"

When the youth hit him he fell sideways, howling, and clutched his ear.

"There", the youth said in a fury, swinging back to them, "you see what you made me do? Come here, Dale, and stop whingeing. Come on. Come on here." But the boy had fled to his mother's skirts and was racked with sobs. The baby shrieked worse than ever. "Jesus", the youth shouted, "you make me sick! Dale", he said, "come here, mate, I didn't mean it, eh? Come here."

The boy met his eye and after a moment moved towards him, still sniffling.

The youth put his hand on the back of the child's neck and drew him in.

"There", he said. "Now, you're not hurt, are you?" The boy, his thumb back in his mouth, leaned into him. The youth sighed.

"Look here", May began. But before she could form another word the youth's arm shot out, an edge of metal struck her, and "Oh God", she said as she went down.

"That's enough out of you", the youth was yelling. "That's the last you get to say."

She thought Harry was about to move, and she put out her hand to stop him.

"No, no", she shouted, "don't. It's all right – I'm all right." The youth, in a kind of panic now, was pushing the gun into the soft of Harry's belly. May, on her knees, tasted salt, put her fingers to her mouth and felt blood.

"All right, now", the youth was saying. He was calming himself, he calmed. But she could smell his sweat. "You can get up now. We're going outside." She looked up then and saw that it made no difference that he was calm. That there was a baby here and that the mother was concerned to get it to sleep. Or that he was so clean-looking, and strict.

She got to her feet without help and went past him on her own legs, though wobbling a little, down the one step into the dark.

The tropical night they had stepped into had a softness that struck Harry like a moment out of his boyhood.

There were stars. They were huge, and so close and heavy-looking that you wondered how they could hold themselves up.

It seemed so personal, this sky. He thought of stepping out as a kid to take a piss from the back verandah and as he sent his jet this way and that looking idly for Venus, or Aldebaran, or the Cross. I could do with a piss right now, he thought, I really need it. It's what I got up for.

They were like little mirrors up there. That's what he had sometimes thought as he came out in the winter dark to load up for his round. If you looked hard enough, every event that was being enacted over all this side of the earth, even the smallest, would be reflected there. Even this one, he thought.

He took May's hand and she clutched his hard. He felt her weight go soft against him.

The youth was urging them on over rough terrain towards a patch of darker scrub further in from the road. Sometimes behind them, but most often half turned and waiting ahead, he could barely contain his impatience at their clumsiness as, heavy and tender-footed, they moved at a jolting pace over the stony ground. When May caught her nightie on a thorn and Harry tried to detach it, the youth made a hissing sound and came back and ripped it clear.

No words passed between them. Harry felt a terrible longing to have the youth speak again, say something. Words you could measure. You knew where they were tending. With silence you were in the open with no limits. But when the fellow stopped at last and turned and stood waiting for them to catch up, it wasn't a particular point in the silence that they had come to. A place thirty yards back might have done equally well, or thirty or a hundred yards further on.

Harry saw with clarity that the distance the youth had been measuring had to do with his reluctance to get to the point, and was in himself.

The gun hung at the end of his arm. He seemed drained now of all energy.

"All right", he said hoarsely, "this'll do. Over here."

It was May he was looking at.

"Yes" he told her. "You."

Harry felt her let go of his hand then, as the youth had directed, but knew she had already parted from him minutes back, when she had begun, with her lips moving in silence, to pray. She took three steps to where the youth was standing, his face turned away now, and Harry stretched his hand out towards her.

"May", he said, but only in his head.

It was the beginning of a sentence that if he embarked on it, and were to say all he wanted her to know and understand in justification of himself and of what he felt, would have no end. The long tale of his inadequacies. Of resolutions unkept, words unspoken, demands whose crudeness, he knew, had never been acceptable to her but which for him were one form of his love – the most urgent, the most difficult. Little phrases and formulae that were not entirely without meaning just because they were common and had been so often repeated.

She was kneeling now, her nightie rucked round her thighs. The youth leaned towards her. Very attentive, utterly concentrated. Her fingers touched the edge of his pineapple shirt.

Harry watched immobilized, and the wide-eyed, faraway look she cast back at him recalled something he had seen on television, a baby seal about to be clubbed. An agonized cry broke from his throat.

But she was already too far off. She shook her head, as if this were the separation she had all this time been warning him of. Then went back to him.

He leaned closer and for a moment they made a single

figure. He whispered something to her that Harry, whose whole being strained towards it, could not catch.

The report was sharp, close, not loud.

"Mayyeee", Harry cried again, out of a dumb, inconsolable grief that would last now for the rest of his life, and an infinite regret, not only for her but for all those women feeling for the lump in their breast, and the ones who had lost kiddies, and those who had never had them and for that boy sending his piss out in an exuberant stream into the dark, his eyes on Aldebaran, and for the last scene at Todgers, that unruly Eden, which he would never get back now, and for his garden choked with weeds. He meant to hurl himself at the youth. But before he could do so he was lifted clean off his feet by a force greater than anything he could ever have imagined, and rolled sideways among stones that after a moment cut hard into his cheek. They were a surprise, those stones. Usually he was careful about them. Bad for the mower.

He would have flung his arms out then to feel for her comfortable softness in the bed, but the distances were enormous and no fence in any direction.

Her name was still in his mouth. Warm, dark, filling it, flowing out.

The youth stood. He was a swarming column. His feet had taken root in the earth.

Darkness was trembling away from the metal, which was hot and hung down from the end of his arm. The force it contained had flung these two bodies down at angles before him and was pulsing away in circles to the edges of the earth.

He tilted his head up. There were stars. Their living but dead light beat down and fell weakly upon him.

He looked towards the highway. The car. Behind it the caravan. Lou and the kids in a close group, waiting.

He felt too heavy to move. There was such a swarming in him. Every drop of blood in him was pressing against the surface of his skin – in his hands, his forearms with their gorged veins, his belly, the calves of his legs, his feet on the stony ground. Every drop of it holding him by force of gravity to where he stood, and might go on standing till dawn if he couldn't pull himself away.

Yet he had no wish to step on past this moment, to move away from it into whatever was to come.

But the moment too was intolerable. If he allowed it to go on any longer he would be crushed.

He launched himself at the air and broke through into the next minute that was waiting to carry him on. Then turned to make sure that he wasn't still standing there on the spot.

He made quickly now for the car and the group his family made, dark and close, beside the taller darkness of the pine.

March 31, 2000

The Party

By Amit Chaudhuri

The dinner had been arranged for, first, Friday, then Saturday night, and already, by the middle of the week, the preparations had begun. They – the small, nuclear family of father, mother and the son who was equal to an army of a hundred – were going to move from this rather equanamous accommodation to a larger flat in another locality in a couple of weeks, so this would probably be the last party Mrs Sinha-Roy would be hosting for some time. Not that the flat was a small one; in fact, it had spaces they didn't know what do with. But with Mr Sinha-Roy's elevation to Head of Finance a few months ago, there was the technicality that the flat had only two bedrooms, only a technicality, since the bedrooms were huge, but yet a two-bedroom flat was not quite commensurate with the position of a Head of Finance, and more practically, his "entertainment" requirements. From now on, he would be expected to throw larger parties.

The young son, Amal, no more than eight years old, lorded it over the servants – the cook, the bearer, the maid – as the preparations made progress, now entering the disorderly activity of the kitchen, now rushing past or circling the sari-clad, abstracted figure of Mrs Sinha-Roy as if she were some kind of portal. There was an enigmatic aura about him that couldn't be quite pinpointed; as if he weren't just the Head of Finance's son, but as if there resided in him, in some indirect but undeniable way, the hopes and aspirations of the company Mr Sinha-Roy worked for; as if he were in some way its secret and unacknowledged symbol. It wasn't enough that the franchise of happiness the company offered lay in the furniture and the flat and other "perquisites"; and that

Mr Sinha-Roy would, as Head of Finance, have to negotiate large losses and gains. The boy too was part of that loss and gain in a way he didn't quite understand.

"What time's Sinha-Roy's dinner?" asked Mr Gupta, glassy-eyed, scratching his stubble as he cruised that morning down Marine Drive. In the office, he referred to Sinha-Roy as "Sir" or "Mr Sinha-Roy", but in private he derived a careless, imperious pleasure from dropping the awed monosyllabic whisper of the first word or the ingratiating, lisping two syllables of the "Mr". This was one of the small freedoms of "company life"; that, however it may have ingrained itself into you as a religion, you did not have to practise it at home. Driving down Marine Drive, Mr Gupta was a free man; though only in a sense, because the car on whose steering wheel his hands rested was an accessory of the company; both a free-moving object that gave him the illusion of ownership and control, and an accomplice to employment.

"Seven thirty", said Mrs Arati Gupta, brushing aside the filigree of her hair that had blown across her face with the breeze. She was the less sharp, but the more pragmatic, even the wiser, of the two. In a sense, she was the one behind the wheel, always had been, always would be, while he made the protestations and clamour of the engine. "But eight o'clock would be all right, don't you think?" always seeking his agreement, if not permission, at the end of a suggestion.

The palm trees of Marine Drive rushed in the opposite direction like a crowd that was running to meet someone. Only recently, Mrs Gandhi had waved a wand – or was it a cane? – and nationalized all the banks, and substantially reduced foreign shareholdings in "private sector" companies. This was true of the "private sector" company, which manufactured paint, in which Mr Gupta worked; it had been made more "Indian" or true-blooded recently, but its status derived from the fact that it had once, not long ago, had the word "British" in its name (the word had now, with dignity, been dispensed with). The "private sector" found itself uneasily on the cusp of a world that had been left behind and which Mrs Gandhi, reportedly, had set about changing.

"Yes, eight o'clock; I don't want to go too early", he said, taking a bend.

Mrs Gupta said, as if the thought had just come to her:

"Should we take something for them?"

There were, of course, no rules on this matter, of visiting your superior's house on what was after all a social and civilized visit, no rules except when you realized that every form of interaction was permeated by company law, not the sort of company law that Mr Gupta had studied laboriously what seemed not many years ago, but the kind that Arati Gupta had become an avid student of.

"I don't know", said her husband gruffly. "It's not done. People will talk."

"People"; "them"; simple, collective pronouns and nouns that had, however, complex but exclusive gradations in the life they'd made their own. "People" were not only managers, heads of sections, and directors, but their wives too. "Them" had the ability to take on different, often contesting, resonances; right now, it conveyed, at once, both Mr and Mrs Sinha-Roy and the difference between them as individuals.

"What about the son, what about Amal", said Mrs Gupta tranquilly. "We should take him a little something."

It was as if she were testing him; she liked teasing him at times.

"What about Amal!" he said, mimicking her. "He doesn't need anything. Don't be silly!" His face had a special vehemence of emotion, that came into being when he knew he'd be called on to display a fatherliness that he did not possess. Somehow, the boy – the idea of him, not even the boy himself – exhausted him more than anything else.

In the Sinha-Roys' flat, the cook, a dark septuagenarian, woke up from a brief nap to finish frying the little patties he'd set aside for the afternoon. The driver rang the bell and came in holding a bouquet of flowers; and Mrs Sinha-Roy, like a somnambulist in her housecoat, moved from dining table to living-room and back again in the heat of the afternoon, distributing flowers from one vase to another.

The whole day seemed like an eternity to the boy, especially as holiday and party happened to coincide with each other in a chance intermission. He had no homework he needed to attack immediately; instead, he had this sense of a function, a role that had come to him out of nowhere, a calling that he was equal to.

By evening, the guests and colleagues, before they left their houses, had begun to apply the finishing touches: after-shave lotion on the cheeks, the last fold of the sari smoothed till it seemed exactly in place. And, at home, like some unappeasable master of ceremonies, Amal tasted the savouries, which were either brought to him on a plate with a glass of cola, or which he himself chose at random.

The Guptas were, as it happened, the first to arrive; they were obliged to look suitably grateful, because they were to occupy this flat from the 23rd of the month; they needed to put in an appearance before anyone else. On the way, Mrs Gupta had bought herself a fragrant mogra from a girl and put it in her hair. The flat itself was on display; every preparatory movement had stopped, and the drawing-room had a finished look about it, as if a work of art had reached its public, final version.

Gradually, the other guests began to trickle in, the doorbell was rung, and each couple greeted with varying degrees of surprise, recognition, and familial warmth. "Where's Amal?" everyone wanted to know, as if the solution to this party lay not in the social hierarchies it represented, nor in the longer-term destinies it vaguely pointed to, but in where, and who, the boy was. Because the party, after all, was a serious business.

As the party moved on, and the evening darkened outside with the intermittent light of other buildings, Atul Gupta found himself, at nine o'clock, alone and moorless for a few minutes in the corridor, with a drink in his hand. With a sort of tentativeness that was rarely visible but had been reserved for his days in the office, that had been naked then but was apparelled in decent clothes since, he realized that the door not far away from him, in which a bright light was shining and which had been left slightly ajar, was the boy's door. He saw his ambition and fear and curiosity had preceded him here, and was waiting like a shadow outside it. He cleared his throat, and, taking a few steps forward, knocked.

"Come in", said a small voice from within.

Mr Gupta's heart beat a little faster. He pushed the door by the handle; the beast, or god, or mystery, the company's innermost secret, however you chose to view him, was sitting there on the edge of his bed, a glass of cola on the floor before him, a drawing book in his hand. This was the Head of Finance's innermost sanctum, this was where his life and heart beat, and he, assistant company secretary, must, against his own wishes, surrender and bow his head silently before it. On a bright red carpet lay, innocently, three or four Dinky toys, including an overturned truck; stopping near it as if it might go off if he touched it, Mr Gupta said:

"How are you, young man?"

The boy turned to look at him; and Mr Gupta flinched, as if his future, or what little he knew of it, had turned to look at him in that air-conditioned room and judged him; for these were not his boss's eyes, but the eyes that, invisibly, ruled and governed his boss's life. He had not known, before he'd begun, that company life concealed such mysteries; the Managing Director's children were long grown up and lived abroad, in England. It was here, then, that, by default, all that was sweet and virginal and innocent about the company dwelt, a savage whose mind was far removed from adult reasoning and the laws that governed adult life.

"Hello, Uncle Atul", said the boy, without much interest. "I'm fine, thank you."

"May I sit down?" said Mr Gupta, smiling, but feeling as

if he were straining against a hidden door that wouldn't open.

"Yes, Uncle", said Amal, glumly preparing for a conversation.

The man sat at the edge of the bed, as if he'd been told to by a wave of the hand. The company itself had never been so perfunctory with him.

"Nice room you have", he said, uttering a truth in a hapless way that made it sound like a lie.

When, in the past, he'd presented his reports and the relevant taxation figures to his superiors, even the worst-compiled of them had more conviction than his platitude. The question that short-sighted politicians and bureaucrats had been asking of companies such as his – was it worth it, the toothpaste, the colas, the enamel paint, the butter? – was one he suddenly found asking himself. He picked up a Dinky toy and put it down again.

The boy said nothing; then, moving his body towards him, handed him the large drawing book he had in his hands.

"I drew these pictures today", he said quietly, without modesty but without bravado either.

"Oh that's nice!" said Mr Gupta, finding it easier to lie as time wore on, staring at the clumsy figures in blue and yellow, as if they were some sort of cipher, or somehow part of that other, more recalcitrant code he was trying to interpret. He bent his head, almost submissively, and said: "What's this?"

He looked very gravely at a misshapen green creature, obviously an animal in the early days of its evolution, with what looked like the rain falling behind it. It was as if the creature had floated out of nowhere into his immediate vision.

"That's a horse", said the boy, simply. "That's the sky", pointing to the crowded blue strokes.

The man nodded slowly, like one who, without realizing it, had been made more knowledgeable, as indeed he had; what had seemed like clouds in his confused, self-created landscape, massed and obfuscating, were resolving themselves into ordinary shapes and forms.

Not finished, he noted a scarecrow-like figure with large eyes. Cheerfully, as if he were now more adept at this game, he asked:

"What's this?"

The boy picked up the tepid cola from the floor, sipped it, as the man respectfully waited for an answer.

"That's baba", the boy revealed casually.

Mr Gupta started; he felt a secret had been revealed to him that no one else in the company knew. So this was how his father, Gupta's own boss, appeared in the eyes of what was hidden, what lay at the source of questions and solutions that he would not be able to understand. Quickly, he asked, still struggling to put his impulses into words:

"Any pictures of you? Or Ma? Or your friends – your best friend?"

The boy closed the drawing book restlessly; Mr Gupta feared his interview was going to be cut short. The sound of the air-conditioner grew in its confidential presence. But he must continue; having been drawn in, he now felt excluded, as if a promise of something, something concrete, had been suggested to him, and immediately withdrawn. Where was he to go now? And if he did not go on, it would not be the boy, or the company, but himself he would be left to blame. In the end, you became your own accuser.

Not the boy, but a warm breath of air from the corridor interrupted him, as the door opened further and Mrs Sinha-Roy said cheerfully:

"Amal, where have you been? Mrs Mehra wants to see you, and there are others waiting to see you outside."

He turned to see Mrs Sinha-Roy, resplendent in her pink Parsi sari, at the door, and Mrs Mehra, large and solid and smiling behind her, one of the lights overhead shining in her eyes. He knew then that all his years of hard work and preparation and dissembling and dreaming would get him no further than where he was.

"I was talking to Uncle Atul", said the boy, as if this

self-evident fact needed his witness to bring it to conclusion.

June 23, 2000

Here Comes Glad

By Paul Magrs

The photos from that time have turned peculiar. I wish we had pictures for then like people do from the 1950s and 1960s, when everything was sharply defined, black and white, time-less. Ours from the early 1980s have us all with savage red eyes because of the way flashes went off. They're toneless in their grainy, inaccurate colours. There was always a film – a glaucoma – that appeared on them, bathing us in citrus tints. We're forever stuck in that moment of surprise with the colours of our hand-knitted jumpers changed. There are pictures of Mark and me on the swing in the garden with scarlet eyes in chunky-knit turquoise and orange.

Even as old as we were – twelve and eight – we'd go out in the same-coloured jumpers, like members of an evangelical family; an advert for the good life. We both had the same little-boys' haircuts, the same length all the way round, like an E. H. Shepard illustration. Mam would cut our hair laboriously as we knelt on the carpet of the top landing, a towel round our shoulders. She'd bite her lip and angle the heavy kitchen scissors and we'd clench our eyes shut, braced for the click of the blades, the frozen touch of them on the napes of our necks. My hair was still blond and Mark's was a chestnut brown, the same as Mam's. We both had pronounced calf-licks in our fringes, which made the job more difficult.

At that age people were always mistaking me for a girl. I had blue eyes, a touch of baby fat, and I shopped with my Mam. That poor woman in Greggs the bakers with the pop-ping-out eyes made the mistake a few times in a row and I just blushed. Mam had to put her right, which made me blush even more. Outside in the precinct Mam tried to tell me I should be proud; men could be pretty as well. Look at the pop stars, who all wore make-up now. We were carrying plastic bags to the bus stop, struggling along with them on wet flag-stones. Mam wouldn't have one of those tartan shopping bags on wheels: they were for old ladies. We didn't mention the Greggs woman's comments again. I wasn't to be mollified on the androgyny front.

Our Big Nanna, Mam's mam, tended to make things worse. She would be enthusiastic every time we'd had our hair trimmed to a more respectable length. "Now you look like proper boys", she'd go.

"They are proper boys", Mam would say.

"You know what I mean. Not boys with girls' haircuts."

This was my Big Nanna all over. Everything in its proper place.

She turned up after New Year's, a couple of days after the ice water had crashed down the outside wall.

Here comes Glad. Here comes my Big Nanna. Always without warning, always wearing a camel coat with her brown shiny handbag clutched under her bosom: the soul of propriety. Fresh from the Sunderland bus. Often with her best friend, deaf Olive, in tow; Olive, who was always more effu-sive and excitable when she arrived than Glad.

"It's because she's deaf", Glad would say, sitting at the pine bench in the kitchen. "They can show their feelings more." She would give Olive a sucked-lemon look and then start looking around, to see if she could spot something newly bought.

"Ee, our Joy", she'd tut to my Mam. "This is all new, these place mats and cups and what-have-you. It's all spending round here. You'll never have anything saved up. It's always like a shop when you come round here. Everything bally new!"

Olive would want to know what was going on. She was half my Big Nanna's height, with owlish glasses, but her voice was twice as loud and I never quite believed she clocked as little as Glad gave her credit for.

"I said, Olive, that our Joy's always buying new bally stuff! Spending her money!"

"Uh-hoh, uh-hoh", Olive agreed in broad Geordie, and looked at Mam, grinning. "Eee, it's lovely, pet. Lovely to see you and the bairns."

My Big Nanna eased her sheepskin gloves off and stared down into her milkless tea. "I hope this is weak enough for me. And I don't want too many cups this time. Last time I was wanting to wet all the way back on the bus. It took about two hours in the snow last time."

Mam took away the teapot.

We watched Glad test her tea. "Bassy go-go!" she cried, quickly blowing on it. "That's hot! Its scalding, our Joy!"

Mam rolled her eyes. Mark and I were pleased. We always liked it when Glad came out with her explosive shouts of "Sally ha-ha!" and "Bassy go-go". We didn't have a clue where they came from. Mam said it was because, way back, there was black in the family and what Glad was doing was bringing up her ancestral memories. We were fascinated by the idea of her being black.

"She came up from Norfolk during the war", Mam would remind us darkly. "All sorts went on in those remote villages. It was like prehistoric times, even then."

And we'd stare at Glad like she was a creature from another world.

This particular time she'd had a rinse put in her hair, especially for the festive season. Usually she opted to turn her perm a mahogany colour, but this time it had a distinctly reddish tinge. I could see my Mam looking at it, as my Big Nanna loosened and took off her plastic rain hat and dropped it on the table while she waited for her tea to cool.

"You've dyed your hair ginger!" Mam cried, and I could see she was holding back from laughing. Mark and I kept quiet, exchanging a quick glance. This is what we mostly did on visits like this, for a while at least. It was much more fun, just watching the adults.

"Ginger by hang!" Glad shouted out. Her thick eyebrows arched up and her cheeks had flushed scarlet. "You cheeky little thing.

"Ginger!"

Olive continued nodding and smiling. "Oh-hoh", she said. "Eee, aye."

"It's a bit red", mam said. "Russet."

Glad's face was burning scarlet now. We knew her hair dyeing had been a sore spot, since last time, when she'd found her perm had thinned at the crown, where she usually slapped the colour solution first.

"She's calling me ginger, Olive! She's saying I've made myself a gingernut!"

Olive blinked and laughed. "Eee!"

"The cheeky beggar", Glad went on. "What does she know? She dyes her hair as well. She should know mahogany when she sees it." Then she seized up her bag and took out some parcels. "Anyway, I've brung up some sausage rolls and those little cakes from Greggs for you. Mind, don't give me nothing. I can't eat, and we're not stopping long, due it'll be dark and they get them madmen on the buses."

Mam took the paper bags from her.

The kitchen door came open and the dog shot in. Our step-father Charlie stood awkwardly in the frame.

"Charlie", Mam said, "You know she doesn't . . . ."

The dog had flown under the kitchen table and was worrying at Glad's legs.

"Bassy go-go! He'll have me over!"

"Duke!" Charlie shouted gruffly. He was still in his duffel coat with the hood up, the dog's lead in his hands. We all started shouting out "Duke".

"You beggar!" Glad cried. "The bally dog's in my bag! He'll have my knitting all to pieces!"

Charlie ducked under the table to grab him by his collar

and haul him out backwards.

"Eee!" Olive squealed. "What a bonny dog!"

Mam sat down heavily at the bench beside us. "Put him out in the garden, Charlie."

Glad was getting herself aerated. She'd clutched her bag up to her chest and was fiddling with her gloves. She'd never liked dogs much. She watched Charlie drag Duke outside and slam the back door after him, so hard the venetian blinds rattled.

"You should have had him trained right in the first place", Glad said. "If he gets out of the garden he'll be like a bally public menace. You'd have to put him down if he did to a normal person what he did to me."

She was referring to when Duke had been younger and even more feckless; when Glad had tried to get in the house through the garden and he'd thrown himself upon her, rather fondly, I thought, and tried to hump her.

"What a bonny dog!" Olive cried.

"Bonny dog nothing", Glad scowled. "They should be made to prove they can look after them before they have dangerous animals about the place." She sipped her tea. "That's a bit less scalding now."

We all watched, with appalled fascination, as she swirled her milkless tea around in the cup and then sucked on a spoon of molten sugar and smacked her lips. It was quiet as she finished her cup.

"And what's better than one cup of tea?" she asked Mark and me, suddenly brightly. It was one of her favourite lines.

"Two cups of tea!" we chimed.

Mam got up to fetch the teapot back from the side.

Funny she never liked dogs, because she knew all about nature. My Nanna had grown up in the wilds, in Norfolk, and had come North during the war. She was a landgirl who had trooped up to South Shields. (By foot, I imagined, the whole way on bleeding feet, hugging the East Coast, with bombs falling all around her.) She was a girl who had barely returned to the place of her birth: the muggy, prehistoric Fens, where everything was darkness and superstition and smelled of brackish mud.

She had grown up in a village called Hunworth, twenty miles from the cathedral in Norwich (where my great-grandma's bush was on display). And she'd walked miles to school each morning, trudging through grey, green fields or endlessly deep snow. She described how nothing came easy there, in the middle of nowhere. There was a pub and a church, and her father's land. She'd milked Mealy, the old cow, every morning. With the other kids she had picked some kind of long grass and this they would stew up and eat.

"You ate grass?" Mark asked, incredulous.

"You'll eat anything when you're that poor. You'll never know about that, thank goodness. Those days are long gone."

Everything she told us about back then was like a little parable. She would tell us the story and then look as if she wasn't sure what the message was supposed to have been.

That afternoon she told us the tale of the Vicar of Stiffkey, which was a village near hers, closer to the coast and a bit more bijou. The vicar had been the talk of the region in the 1930s: involved in some scandal or other.

"Something I never understood. I was a bairn and we weren't allowed to know all the ins and outs on it. If you ask me, kids these days know too much." She eyed Mark and me. "They know more than their granny. Anyway, the thing was, what he did when he was found out, he ran away to the circus. He did, the beggar! And he started doing this act with a lion. Putting his head in the lion's mouth and what-have-you. And then the bally lion bit his head off! What do you think on that?"

She never tired of telling us how different things were now and how easy we had it. How we got too much. How we'd never come to value anything.

On one of these visits it had come out that in the last election Glad had voted Tory. All of us were shocked. But in the 1980s, Glad was a natural Tory. She'd struggled on her own with four kids and she'd worked hard in service, in munitions factories, in school kitchens. When the offer came to buy your own council house, she was straight in there, sending my grown-up Uncle Richard, who still lived with her, down the council office with a bag containing seven thousand pounds in cash. Help yourself and your own. The world is a nasty place and you can't trust people. Keep yourself to yourself. Everyone's on the make and everything's getting worse. Concentrate on feathering your own nest with whatever you can earn.

She'd brought up two daughters to marry middle-class men – a dentist and an insurance clerk – and move away to the South. And she'd had one son who'd been in the Army for a while and who then came home to stay. And she'd had my Mam, who'd married and had me young and been divorced young.

There was a lot of history there, between Mam and my Big Nanna. Some of it I'd witnessed, some I was still, at twelve, only learning about. I knew they didn't kiss each other or hug. I knew they acted sometimes like polite and wary strangers with each other. There was always a tension between them. It was as if Glad was forever appraising Mam; measuring her up; keeping out a watchful eye.

I knew it drove my Mam up the wall, that beady eye. My Big Nanna would sit there, birdlike, in a blouse with a brooch and a crocheted waistcoat over the top. She sat at the kitchen table and watched Mam deal with tea, cakes, biscuits and it was as if she was watching for mistakes, for any kind of lapse.

It was at this age that I learned – late, I know – to make a perfect cup of tea. Mam hadn't wanted us messing on with kettles. She protected us from everything she could, conscientiously. Maybe even made us – me, at least – impractical at most things. But by twelve I could get up and make tea and be the one who was being watched, doing things. Taking some of the heat off.

I knew we wouldn't sit at the table for the whole visit. If it was a decent day, Glad might want to go for a walk and I would go with her. She thought walking was the best exercise – an almost godly activity. She walked like the Queen, only twice as fast; clip-clopping along in sensible shoes, bag held under her bosom with one hand, the other arm swinging briskly free. On the way, if we were walking along the Burn, among the trees, she'd point out their types and listen for the birdsong: wood pigeons, cuckoos. She knew them all and would stop at the bridge, cock her head and imitate them back.

She'd say: "I've forgotten most on 'em. Forgotten more than I ever knew."

The ice that day would have been no problem. She'd sent off a coupon from an advert in the *Daily Mirror*: bought herself some snow-treads to clamp to her shoes. She pulled them out of her bag and they were fierce, sabre-toothed things with hinges, like mantraps. She slipped her shoes off quickly to show how they attached. She was careful not to put a shoe on the table, that being as unlucky as having bird ornaments about the place.

"Uh-hoh", Olive laughed. "They're smashing, aren't they?"

"Did you send off for some as well, Olive?" Mam shouted.

"Uh-hoh, aye. I did, aye", she laughed.

Glad rolled her eyes. "No, she didn't. She's just saying that to chime in. You couldn't trust her with something like these. Mind, she's always falling over. Aren't you, Olive, hinny? You're always falling over?"

Olive seemed to cotton on. "Oh, aye. I'm always falling over, you bugger." Olive used that lovely, non-personal "you bugger" in the proper broad Geordie way: not calling anyone, just a generalized and fond stab at the world at large.

"She's a danger to herself. She goes round laughing all the time and not watching where she's going", Glad said. "Aren't you?"

"Aye, aye. I am."

Time to retire to the front room for a bit, to sit on the settee with knitting and a further cup of tea.

Mam led the way, almost apologizing for the decorations still being up. We had an artificial tree with the fairy old as me on top, and swags of tinsel on the walls, carrying all the cards.

"I wanted to take it down on New Year's Day", Mam said. "The bairns wouldn't let me. I hate all the clutter once Christmas is over. I want to be back to normal."

Glad looked at the tree. "It's the first time I've seen your tree this Christmas."

That was about not being invited down.

"And you never got to see mine", she added. Another dig, about our not going to hers on Boxing Day. Her tree was always the same anyway. A threadbare silver affair on a green stand with tinsel so ratty and sharp it looked as if it could cut you to ribbons if you touched it out of turn. All the ornaments were like glass shells, sprayed silver. Something about that tree always made me sad. It looked terribly flammable, or as if it had already been mostly singed away.

"I took ours – mine and Richard's – down on New Year's Eve." Glad didn't think much of New Year's Eve. It was an excuse for those who drank to go out and go on daft. To act how they wanted. I'd only seen her drink a couple of times. A few delicate sips of sherry, kept in the sideboard and turned to molten sugar with age. She would get those two red spots on her cheeks, just like she did when she was being quietly furious.

Charlie disappeared, Mark disappeared and I followed the ladies to the living room, where Olive and Glad took out their knitting, once they were comfortable on the settee. Mam perched herself on the armchair and tugged her Redicut box towards her. As the clicking from the ladies' needles began – a busy, consoling sound – Mam looked almost shy about pulling out her canvas with the tiger half-done.

"You've got this room lovely", Olive said. "Lovely, pet."

Mam smiled and hefted out the tiger tapestry.

"Eee!" Olive cried. "You bugger, look at that!"

Glad was taking her glasses out of her case. She put them on and peered over the top of them, her mouth pursed. "What the devil's that meant to be, then?"

"It's a tiger!" bellowed Olive.

Glad stared at the Bengal tiger: straight in the eye. She looked down at the bobble hat she was on with. "Aye, well. They're always thinking of something new. Something to keep you spending your money."

They fell quiet then. Mam looked down at her Redicut rug, took a big sigh, and started tagging the wool on.

"Mam", I said, "Tell them about the other night. About how all the ice water fell off our roof into next door's house . . . and about how that wife next door went mad in her hairnet."

"What's this?" Glad asked, avid for trouble.

"Well", Mam said, and then she was off, telling the whole tale.

Glad listened and tutted, especially when it came to hearing about how the water had gone through the little boy Leighton's bedroom, which happened to be the cupboard at the top of the stairs. "Fancy keeping the bairn in a cupboard."

Then she countered with a story of her own, about being at the bingo in South Shields and being cold-shouldered by my dad's parents. My Little Nanna and Granda had turned up dressed to the nines and had studiously ignored her. The old man had made a show of pulling up a chair for my Little Nanna. "Silly old fool", Glad said. "He's like her slave. They go rubbing everyone's nose in it. Waving hello to people like they're famous. And she still dresses far too young."

I felt sick every time Glad mentioned having seen them out. Mark and I hadn't seen them for about two years. That was a finished chapter.

Mam and Glad went on trading stories, repeating the dialogue, doing the voices, imitating every quirk and gesture. They always did this. And I was always agog. I sat listening and Olive knitted – booties for a friend's niece – and she would pitch in with random "Uh-hoh"s.

But my Mam and Glad talked and talked up a storm.

Afterwards, later that night, Mam would say, out of the blue: "I don't know. I just can't talk to her." She was washing up the tea plates, staring out of the window, over the terraced roofs opposite. "I just have nothing to say to her."

This was after they'd gone, after I'd taken a little walk with my Big Nanna in the lowering gloom. Her snow grips clicked on the ice as we clipped along.

"You have to look after your mam, Paul. Make sure you always do."

She looked down at me as we walked to the edge of the estate. She nodded to one house in particular, one I knew well. "Ah, that was Charlie's parents' house, wasn't it? That poor old man. He was a proper gentleman. He was proud of Charlie, meeting your mam. Well, now they haven't got Charlie's mam and dad nearby." It was true; Arthur had died the year before and Rini, Charlie's mam, had gone back to Australia. Someone else was in their house and the horse brasses would be down, the nicotined ceilings painted over.

We walked steadily by the white field, the berried hedgerows, and the street lights were starting to come on, pink, then yellow.

"I've always tried to look out for your mam", Glad said. "She's the most sensitive one of all of them, you know. All my bairns. Her dad, your grandad-as-would-have been; he knew that. She was nine when he died. When he was in that place at the end, that was one of the last things he said to me. 'You have to watch out for our Joy. She's the best one of the lot. Out of all of them, she's the best.'" We went along a little more, and then started heading back. Glad and Olive would have to catch their bus north soon.

She glanced at me, appraisingly and as if to impress what she was saying onto me. "So you have to look after her, Paul. I've tried. I still try. But . . . ."

She didn't go on. I watched both our breaths – healthy, deep, walking breaths – dissipate and fog as the cold stole in.

One of Mark's Christmas presents had been a Polaroid camera. He'd come down to say goodbye to them, fully armed with flashbulbs and film.

We all crouched on the living-room floor, in front of the Christmas tree. Olive made us squash together and grin. She would bark out laughing and then look along, to check that everyone else was doing the same.

Glad said, "She's always laughing. She doesn't care, does she?"

The rest of us were always self-conscious in front of cameras. Mark wasn't, at that age. He held up Star Wars figures, showing them off; a Stormtrooper and a Tusken Raider as Mam hugged him for a picture.

"Olive always comes out well on bally snaps", Glad said. "It's because she doesn't care how she looks."

"Smile!" Olive laughed. "Everyone smile, you bugger!"

We did, and we watched each other's print develop slowly; the blues, yellows and greens rising out of the flat grey, once the camera had clicked, whirred and flashed. All of us had bright red eyes.

September 7, 2001

Curved is the Line of Beauty

By Hilary Mantel

Before you can speak, even before you take your first steps outside your house, there is a moment when you are lost or
found. It's a matter of language, accent, the current of the air,
and those accidents that identify us – or not – with the place,
the time, the people around us. There are places that enclose
you and places that leave you scalped by the knife of the wind;
there are places that have "lost" inscribed on them, scrawled
over their grid reference in invisible ink. I have always
understood that the chances of being lost were high, because I
was born on the edge of the moors, and grew up on stories of
its murderous ways. Moorland punished those who were
stupid and those who were unprepared. Ramblers from
Manchester, slack-jawed boys with bobble hats, would walk
for days in circles, till they died of exposure; and clammy fogs,
like sheets drawn over corpses, would thwart the rescue
parties. Moorland was featureless except for its own swell and
eddy, its slow waves of landscape rising and falling, its knolls,
streams and bridle paths which ran between nowhere and
nowhere; its wetness underfoot, its scaly patches of late snow,
and the tossing inland squall that was its typical climate. In
calm weather, its air was wandering, miasmic, like memories
that no one owns. When I was about ten years old, children of
my age began to disappear from the milltown conurbations
and the Manchester backstreets. It was in moorland that their
bodies were found; one at least is unrecovered. England had
not thought there were places like these: beyond the metro-
politan imagination, out of range of compass and map.

The other way of being lost, when I was a child, was by

being damned. Damned to hell that is, for all eternity. This could happen very easily if you were a Catholic child in the 1950s. If the speeding driver caught you at the wrong moment – let us say, at the midpoint between monthly Confessions – then your soul could part from your body in such a blackened state that you would never see the face of God. Our school was situated handily, so as to increase the risks, between two bends in the road. Last-moment repentance is possible, and stress was placed on it. You might be saved if, in your final welter of mashed bones and gore, you remembered the formula. So it was really all a matter of timing. I didn't think it might be a matter of mercy. Mercy was a theory that I had not seen in operation. I had only seen how those who wielded power extracted maximum advantage from every situation. The politics of the playground and classroom are as instructive as those of the parade-ground and the senate. I understood that, as Thucydides would later tell me, "the strong exact what they can, and the weak yield what they must".

Accordingly, if the strong said "we are going to Birmingham", to Birmingham you must go. We were going to make a visit, to a family we had not met, and in the days after the announcement I said the word "family" many times to myself, its crumbly soft sound like a rusk in milk, and I carried its scent with me, the human warmth of chequered blankets and the yeast smell of babies' heads. In the week before the visit, I went over in my head the circumstances that surrounded it, challenged myself with a few contradictions and puzzles which they threw up, and analysed who "us" might be, because that was not a constant or a simple matter.

The night before the visit, I was sent to bed at eight, even though it was the holidays and Saturday next day. I opened the sash window and leaned out into the dusk, waiting till a lonely string of streetlights blossomed, far over the fields, under the upland shadow. There was a sweet grassy fragrance, a haze in the twilight; Dr Kildare's Friday night theme tune floated out from a hundred TV sets, from a hundred open windows and doors, up the hill, across the reservoir and over the moors, and as I fell asleep I saw the medics in their frozen poses, fixed, solemn and glazed, like heroes on the curve of an antique jar.

I once read of a jar on which this verse was engraved:

Straight is the line of duty;
Curved is the line of beauty.
Follow the straight line; thou shalt see
The curved line ever follow thee.

At five o'clock, a shout roused me from my dreams. I went downstairs in my blue spotted pyjamas to wash in hot water from the kettle, and I saw the outline of my face, puffy, in the light like grey linen tacked to the summer window. I had never been so far from home; even my mother had never, she said, been so far. I was excited and excitement made me sneeze. My mother stood in the kitchen in the first uncertain shaft of sun, making sandwiches with cold bacon and wrapping them silently, sacramentally, in grease-proof paper.

We were going in Jack's car, which stood the whole night, these last few months, at the kerb outside our house. It was a small grey car, like a jellymould, out of which a giant might turn a foul jelly of profanity and grease. The car's character was idle, vicious and sneaky. If it had been a pony you would have shot it. Its engine fizzed most days and steamed, its underparts rattled; it wanted brake shoes and new exhausts. It jibbed at hills and sputtered to a halt on bends. It ate oil and when it wanted a new tyre there were rows about having no money, and slamming the doors so hard that the glass of the kitchen cupboard rattled in its grooves.

The car brought out the worst in everybody who saw it. It was one of the first cars on the street, and the neighbours, in their mistaken way, envied it. Already sneerers and ill-wishers of ours, they were driven to further spite when they saw us trooping out to the kerb carrying all the rugs and kettles and camping stoves and raincoats and wellington boots that we took with us for a day at the seaside or the zoo.

There were five of us, now. Me and my mother; two biting, snarling, pinching little boys; Jack. My father did not go on our trips. Though he still slept in the house – the room down the corridor, the one with the ghost – he kept to his own timetables and routines, his Friday jazz club and his solitary sessions of syncopation, picking at the piano, late weekend afternoons, with a remote gaze. This had not always been his way of life. He had once taken me to the library. He had taken me out with my fishing net. He had taught me card games and how to read a race-card; it might not have been a suitable accomplishment for an eight-year-old, but any skill at all was a grace in our dumb old world.

But those days were now lost to me. Jack had come to stay with us. At first he was just a visitor and then without transition he seemed to be always there. He never carried in a bag, or unpacked clothes; he just came complete as he was. After his day's work he would drive up in the evil car, and when he came up the steps and through the front door, my father would melt away to his shadowy evening pursuits. Jack had a brown skin and muscles beneath his shirt. He was your definition of a man, if a man was what caused alarm and shattered the peace. To amuse me while my mother combed the tangles out of my hair, he told me the story of David and Goliath.

It was not a success. He tried his hardest, as I tried also, to batten down my shrieks. As he spoke his voice slid in and out of the London intonations with which he had been born; his brown eyes flickered, caramel and small, the whites jaundiced. He made the voice of Goliath, but – to my mind – he was lacking in the David department.

After a long half hour, it was over. My vast weight of hair studded to my skull with steel clips, I pitched exhausted from my kitchen chair. Jack stood up, equally exhausted, I suppose; he would not have known how often this needed to happen. He liked children, or imagined he did. But owing to recent events and my cast of mind, I was not exactly a child, and he himself was a very young man, too inexperienced to navigate through the situation in which he had placed himself, and he was always on the edge, under pressure, chippy and paranoid and quick to take offence. I was afraid of his flaring temper and his irrationality: he argued with brute objects, kicked out at iron and wood, cursed the fire when it wouldn't light. I flinched at the sound of his voice, but I kept the flinch inwards. Nothing was readable on my tiny features, except the traces of ineradicable contempt.

When I look back now I feel – insofar as I can read my feelings – a faint stir of fellow feeling that is on the way to pity. The writer Gail Godwin says that "behind every story that begins 'When I was a child' there exists another story in which adults are fighting for their lives".

It was Jack's quickness of temper, and his passion for the underdog, that was the cause of our trip to Birmingham. We were going to see a friend of his, who was from Africa. You will remember that we have barely reached the year 1962, and I had never seen anyone from Africa, except in photographs, but the prospect in itself was less amazing to me than the knowledge that Jack had a friend. I thought friends were for children. My mother seemed to think that you grew out of them. Adults did not have friends. They had relatives. Only relatives came in your house. Neighbours might come, of course. But not to our house. My mother was now the subject of scandal and did not go out. We were all the subject of scandal, but some of us had to. I had to go to school, for instance. It was the law.

It must have been six o'clock when we bundled into the car, the two little boys dropped sleep-stunned beside me on to the red leather of the back seat. In those days it took a very long time to get anywhere. There were no motorways to speak of. Fingerposts were still employed, and we did not seem to have the use of a map. Because my mother did not know left from right, she would cry "That way, that way!" whenever she saw a sign and happened to read it. The car would swerve off in any old direction and Jack would start cursing and she would shout back. Our journeys usually found us bogged in the sand at Southport, or broken down by the drystone wall of some Derbyshire beauty spot, the lid of the vile spitting engine propped open, my mother giving advice from the wound-down window; fearful advice, which went on till Jack danced with rage on the roadway, or the uncertain sand, his voice piping in imitation of a female shriek, and she, heaving up the last rags of self-control, heaving them into her arms like some dying soprano's bouquet, would drop her voice an octave and claim "I don't talk like that."

But on this particular day, we didn't get lost at all. It seemed a miracle. At the blossoming hour of ten o'clock, the weather still fine, we ate our sandwiches, and I remember that first sustaining bite of salted fat, sealing itself in a plug to the hard palate; the sip of Nescafé to wash it down, poured steaming from the flask. In some town we stopped for petrol. That too passed without incident. I rehearsed, in my mind, the reason behind the visit. The man from Africa, the friend, was not now but had once been a workmate of Jack's. And they had spoken. And his name was Jacob. My mother had told me, don't say "Jacob is black" say "Jacob is coloured". What, coloured? I said. What, striped? Like the threadbare towel which, at that very moment, was hanging to dry before the fire? I stared at it, washed to a patchy pink-grey. I felt it; the fibres were stiff as dried grass. Black, my mother said, is not the term polite people use. And stop mauling that towel.

So now, the friend, Jacob. He had married a white girl. They had gone to get lodgings. They had been turned away. The stable door bolted. Though Eva was expecting. Especially because she was expecting. NO COLOUREDS, the signs said. Oh, merrie England! At least people could spell in those days. They didn't write NO COLOURED'S or "NO" COLOUREDS. That's about all you can say for it.

So: Jacob unfolded to Jack this predicament of his: no

house, the insulting notices, the pregnant Eva. Jack, quickly taking fire, wrote a letter to a newspaper. The newspaper, quick to spot a cause, took fire also. There was naming and shaming; there was a campaign. Letters were written and questions were asked. The next thing you knew, Jacob had moved to Birmingham, to a new job. There was a house now, a baby, indeed two. Better days were here. But Jacob would never forget how Jack had taken up the cudgels. That, my mother said, was the phrase he had used. David and Goliath, I thought. My scalp prickled, and I felt steel pins cold against it. Last night had been too busy for the combing. My hair fell smoothly down my back, but hidden above the nape of my neck there was a secret pad of fuzziness which, if slept on one more night, would require a howling hour to unknot.

The house of Jacob was built of brick in a quiet colour, with a white-painted gate and a tree in a tub outside. One huge window stared out at a grass verge, with a sapling; and the road curved away, lined with similar houses, each in their own square of garden. We stepped out of the heat of the car and stood jelly-legged on the verge. Behind the plate glass was a stir of movement, and Jacob opened the front door to us, his face breaking into a smile. He was a tall slender man, and I liked the contrast of his white shirt with the soft sheen of his skin. I tried hard not to say, even to think, the term that is not the one polite people use. Jacob, I said to myself, is quite a dark lavender, verging on purple on an overcast day.

Eva came out from behind him. She had a compensatory pallor, and when she reached out, vaguely patting at my little brothers, she did it with fingers like rolled dough. Well, well, the adults said. And, this is all very nice. Lovely, Eva. And fitted carpets. Yes, said Eva. And would you like to go and spend a penny? I didn't know this phrase. Wash your hands, my mother said. Eva said, up you run, poppet. At the top of the stairs there was a bathroom, not an arrangement I had reason to take for granted. Eva ushered me into it, smiling, and clicked the door behind her. There was a bolt on it and I thought for a moment of bolting myself in. Standing at the basin and watching myself in the mirror, I washed my hands carefully with Camay soap. Maybe I was dehydrated from the journey, for I didn't seem to need to do anything else. I hummed to myself, "You'll look a little lovelier . . . each day . . . with fabulous Camay." I didn't look around much. I dried carefully between my fingers with the towel behind the door. Already I could hear them on the stairs, shouting that it was their turn.

Everything had been fine, till the last hour of the journey. "Not long to go", my mother had said, and suddenly swivelled in her seat. She watched us, silent, her neck craning. Then she said, "When we are visiting Jacob, don't say 'Jack'. It's not suitable. I want you to say", and here she began to struggle with her words, "Daddy . . . Daddy Jack."

Her head, once more, faced front. Studying the curve of her cheek, I thought she looked sick. It had been a most unconvincing performance. I was almost embarrassed for her. "Is this just for today?" I asked. My voice came out cold. She didn't answer.

When I got back into the downstairs room they were parading Eva's children, a toddler and a baby, and remarking that it was funny how it came out, so you had one butter-coloured and one blueish, and Jacob was saying, too, that it was funny how it came out and you couldn't ever tell, really, it was probably beyond the scope of science as we know it today. The sound of a pan rocking on the gas jet came from the kitchen, and there was a burst of wet steam, and some clanking; Eva said carrots, can't take your eye off them. Wiping her hands on her apron, she made for the door and melted into the steam. My eyes followed her. Jacob smiled and said, so how is the man who took up the cudgels?

We children ate in the kitchen – us, that is, because the two babies sat in their own high chairs by Eva and sucked gloop from a spoon. There was a little red table with a hinged flap, and Eva propped the back door open so that the sunlight from the garden came in. We had thick pale slices of roast pork, and gravy that was beige and so thick it kept the shape of the knife. Probably if I am honest about what I remember I think it is the fudge texture of this gravy that stays in my mind, better even than the afternoon's choking panic, the tears and prayers that were now only an hour or so away.

After our dinner Tabby came. She was not a cat but a girl, and the niece of Jacob. Enquiries were made of me: did I like to draw? Tabby had brought a large bag with her, and from it she withdrew sheets of rough coloured paper and a whole set of coloured pencils, double-ended. She gave me a quick, modest smile, and a flicker of her eyes. We settled down in a corner, and began to make each other's portrait.

Out in the garden the little boys grubbed up worms, shrieked, rolled the lawn with each other and laid about them with their fists. I thought that the two coloured babies, now snorting in milky sleep, would be doing the same thing before long. When one of the boys fetched the other a harder clout than usual, the victim would howl "Jack! Jack!"

My mother stood looking over the garden. "That's a lovely shrub, Eva", she said. I could see her through the angle made by the open door of the kitchen; her high-heeled sandals planted four-square on the lino. She was smaller than I had thought, when I saw her beside the floury bulk of Eva, and her eyes were resting on something further than the shrub: on the day when she would leave the moorland village behind her, and have a shrub of her own. I bent my head over the paper and attempted the blurred line of Tabby's cheek, the angle of neck to chin. The curve of flesh, its soft bloom, eluded me; I lolled my pencil point softly against the paper, feeling I wanted to roll it in cream, or in something vegetable-soft but tensile, like the the fallen petal of a rose. I had already noticed, with interest, that Tabby's crayons were sharpened down in a similar pattern to the ones I had at home. There was little call for gravy colour and even less for bl . . . k. Most popular with her was gold/green: as with me. Least popular: morbid mauve/dark pink. Those days when I gave up crayoning, and started to play that the crayons were soldiers, I had to imagine that gold/green was a drummer boy, so short was he.

My pencil snagged. This paper is for kids, I thought. An obscure insult, trailing like the smell of old vegetable water, seemed to hang in the air. My fingers clenched. Fired by a spurt of rage, my wrist stiffening, I ripped into the paper. My pencil, held like a dagger, tore at its surface. At my toppest speed, I began to execute cartoon men, with straight jointless limbs, with blown "O"s for heads, with wide grinning mouths, jug ears; petty Goliaths with slatted mouths, with five finger-bones splaying from their wrists. Tabby looked up. Shh, shh . . . she said; as if soothing me. I drew children rolling in the grass, children made of two circles with a third "O" for their bawling mouths. Jacob came in, laughing, talking over his shoulder, ". . . so I tell him, if you want a trained draughtman for £6 a week, man, you can whistle for him!" I thought, I won't call him anything, I won't give him a name. I'll nod my head in his direction so they'll know who I mean. I'll even point to him, though polite people don't point. Daddy Jack! Daddy Jack! They can whistle for him!

Jacob stood over us, smiling softly. The crisp turn of his collar, the top button released, disclosed his velvet quite dark-coloured throat. "Two nice girls", he said. "What have we here?" He picked up my paper. "Talent!" he said. "Did you do this, sweetheart, by yourself?" He was looking at the cartoon men, not my portrait of Tabby, those tentative strokes in the corner of the page: not the curve of her jaw, like a note in music. "Hey, Jack", he said, "now this is good, I can't believe it at her young age." I whispered "I am nine", as if I wanted to alert him to the true state of affairs. Jacob waved the paper around, delighted. "I could well say this is a prodigy", he said. I turned my face away. It seemed indecent to look at him. In that one moment it seemed to me that the world was blighted, and that every adult throat bubbled, like a garbage pail in August, with the syrup of rotting lies.

I see them, now, from the car window, children any day, on any road; children going somewhere, disconnected from the routes of adult intent. You see them in trios or pairs, in unlikely combinations, sometimes a pair with a little one tagging along, sometimes a boy with two girls. They carry, it might be, a plastic bag with something secret inside, or a stick or box, but no obvious plaything; sometimes a ratty dog processes behind them. Their faces are intent and their missions hidden from adult eyes; they have a geography of their own, urban or rural, that has nothing to do with the milestones and markers that adults use. The country through which they move is older, more intimate than ours. They have their private knowledge of it. You do not expect this knowledge to fail.

There was no need to ask if we were best friends, me and Tabby, as we walked the narrow muddy path by the water. Perhaps it was a canal, but a canal was not a thing I'd seen, and it seemed to me more like a placid inland stream, silver-grey in colour, tideless not motionless, fringed by sedge and tall grasses. My fingers were safely held in the pad of Tabby's palm, and there was a curve of light on the narrow, coffee-coloured back of her hand. She was a head taller than me, willowy, cool to the touch, even at the hot end of this hot afternoon. She was ten and a quarter years old, she said, almost as if it were something to shrug away. In her free hand she held a paper bag, and in this bag – which she had taken from her satchel, her eyes modestly downcast – were ripe plums.

They were – in their perfect dumpling under my finger tips, in their cold purple blush – so fleshy that to notch your teeth against their skin seemed like becoming a tea-time cannibal, a vampire for the day. I carried my plum in my palm, caressing it, rolling it like a dispossessed eye, and feeling it grow warm from the heat of my skin. We strolled, so; till Tabby pulled at my hand, stopped me, and turned me towards her, as if she wanted a witness. She clenched her hand. She rolled the dark fruit in her fist, her eyes on mine. She raised her fist to her sepia mouth. Her small teeth plunged into ripe flesh. Juice ran down her chin. Casually she wiped it. She turned her face full to mine, and for the first time I saw her frank smile, her lips parted, the gap between her teeth at the front. She flipped my wrist lightly, with the back of her fingers; I felt the sting of her nails. "Let's go on the wrecks", she said.

It meant we must scramble through a fence. Through a gap there. I knew it was illicit. I knew no would be said but then what, this afternoon, did I care for no? Under the wire, through the snag of it, the gap already widened by the hands of forerunners, some of whom must have worn double-thick-ness woollen double-knit mittens, to muffle the scratch against their flesh. Once through the wire, Tabby went, "Whoop!"

Then soon she was bouncing, dancing in the realm of the dead cars. They were above our head to the height of three. Her hands reached out to flip at their rusting door-sills and wings. If there had been glass in their windows, it was strewn now at our feet. Scrapes of car-paint showed, fawn, banana, a degraded scarlet. I was giddy, and punched my fingers at metal; it crumbled, I was through it. For that moment only I may have laughed; but I do not think so.

She led me on the paths to the heart of the wrecks. We play here, she said, and towed me on. We stopped for a plum each. We laughed. "Are you too young to write a letter?" she asked. I did not answer. "Have you heard of penfriends? I have one already."

All around us, the scrap-yard showed its bones. The wrecks stood clear now, stack on stack, against a declining yellow light. When I looked up they seemed to foreshorten, these carcasses, and bear down on me; gaping windows where faces looked out once, empty engine cavities where the air was blue, treadless tyres, wheel arches gaping, boots unsprung and empty of bags, unravelling springs where seats were once; and some wrecks were warped, reduced, as if by fire, bl . . . kened. We walked, sombre, cheeks bulging, down the paths between. When we had penetrated, many rows in, by blind corners, by the swerves enforced on us by the squishy corrosion of the sliding piles, I wanted to ask, why do you play here and who is you, and also can we go now please?

Tabby ducked out of sight, around some rotting heap. I heard her giggle. "Got you!" I said. "Yes!" She ducked, shying away, but my plum stone hit her square on the temple, and as it touched her flesh I tasted the seducing poison which, if you crack a plum stone, your tongue can taste. Then Tabby broke into a trot, and I chased her: when she skidded to a halt, her flat brown sandals making brakes for her, I stopped too, and glanced up, and saw we had come to a place where I could hardly see the sky. Have a plum, she said. She held the bag out. I am lost, she said. We are, we are, lost. I'm afraid to say.

What came next I cannot, you understand, describe in clock-time. I have never been lost since, not utterly lost, without the sanctuary of sense; without the reasonable hope that I will and can and deserve to be saved. But for that next buried hour, we ran like rabbits, pile to pile, scrap to scrap, the wrecks that had become our total world towering, as we went deeper, for twenty feet above our heads. I could not blame her. I did not. But I did not see how I could help us either. If it had been the moors, some ancestral virtue would have propelled me, I felt, towards the metalled road, towards a stream bed or cloud that would have conveyed me, soaked and beaten, towards the A57, towards the sanctity of some strangers' car; and the wet inner breath of that vehicle would have felt to me, whoever owned it, like the wet protective breathing of the belly of the whale.

But here, there was nothing alive. There was nothing I could do, for there was nothing natural. The metal stretched, friable, bl . . . k, against evening light. We shall have to live on plums for ever, I thought. For I had the sense to realize that the only excursion here would be from the wreckers' ball. No flesh would be sought here; there would be no rescue team.

When Tabby reached for my hand, her fingertips were cold as ball-bearings. Once, she heard people calling. Men's voices. She said she did. I heard only distant, formless shouts. They are calling our names, she said. Jacob, Jack. They are calling for us.

She began to move, for the first time, in a purposive direction. In her eyes was that shifty light of unconviction, that I had seen on my mother's face – could it be only this morning? A scalding pair of tears popped into my eyes. To know that I lived, I touched the knotted mass of hair, the secret above my nape: my fingers rubbed and rubbed it, round and round. If I survived, it would have to be combed out, with torture. This seemed to militate against life; and then I felt, for the first time and not the last, that death at least is straightforward. Tabby stopped, her breath tight and short, and held out to me the last plum stone, the kernel, sucked clear of flesh. I took it without disgust from her hand. Tabby's troubled eyes looked at it. It sat in my palm, a shrivelled brain from some small animal. Tabby leaned forward. She was still breathing hard. The edge of her littlest nail picked at the convolutions. She put her hand against her ribs. She said, "It is the map of the world."

There was an interval of praying. I will not disguise it. It was she who raised the prospect. "I know a prayer", she said. I waited. "Little Jesus, meek and mild . . . ." I said "What's the good of praying to a baby?"

She threw her head back. Her nostrils flared. Prayers began to run out of her. "Now I lay me down to sleep . . . ." Stop, I said. "If I should die before I wake . . . ."

My fist, before I even knew it, clipped her across the mouth.

After a time, she raised her hand there. Her fingers trembled against the corner of her lip, the crushed flesh like velvet, creeping it down for a moment so that the darker membrane showed. There was no blood. I said, "Aren't you going to cry?" She said, "Are you?" I couldn't say, I never cry. It was not true. She knew it. She said softly, it is all right if you want to cry. Don't you know a Catholic prayer?

Hail Mary. I said. She said, Teach it me. And I could see why, because the sun lay in angry streaks across farther peaks of the junk yard. "Don't you have a watch?" she whispered. "I have one, but it is at home, in my bedroom", I said. I have a watch it is a Westclox, but I am not allowed to wind it, it is only to be wound by Jack. I wanted to say, and often he is tired, it is late, my watch is winding down, it is stopping but I dare not ask, and when next day it's stopped there's bellowing, only I can do a bleeding thing in this bleeding house. (Door slam.)

There is a certain prayer which never fails. It is to St Bernard; or by him, I was never quite clear. Remember oh most loving, further adjectives, mother of god/virgin etc, that it is a thing unheard of that anyone ever, beseeched thy aid, sought thy intercession or implored thy help and was left forsaken. I thought that I had it, close enough, the beseech and besought of it; could a few errors matter, when you were kicking at the Immaculate's gate? I was ready to implore: and it was the most powerful prayer ever invented. It was a clear declaration that heaven must help you or go to hell. It was a taunt, a challenge, to Holy Mary Mother Of God. Get it fixed! Do it now! It is a thing unheard of! But just as I was about to begin, I realized I must not say it after all. Because if it didn't work . . . .

The strength seemed to drain away then, from my arms and legs. I sat down, in the deep shadow of the wrecks, when all the indications were that we should keep climbing. I wasn't about to take a bet on St Bernard's prayer, and live my life knowing it was useless. I must have thought there were worse circumstances, in which I'd need to deal this last card from my sleeve. "Climb!" said Tabby. I climbed. I knew – did she? – that the rust might crumble beneath us and drop us into the heart of the wrecks. Climb, she said, and I did: each step tested, so that I learned the resistance of rotting metal, the play and the give beneath my feet, the pathetic cough and wheeze of it, its abandonment and ferrous despair. Tabby climbed. Her feet scurried, light, skipping, the soles of her sandals skittering and scratching like rats. And then, like stout Cortez, she stopped, stared. "The woodpiles!" I gazed upwards into her face. She swayed and teetered, six feet above me. Evening breeze whipped her skirt around her stick-legs. "The woodpiles!" Her face opened like a flower.

What she said meant nothing to me, but I understood the message. We are out! she cried. Her arm beckoned me. Come on, come on! She was shouting at me, but I was crying too hard to hear. I worked myself up beside her: crab arms, crab legs, two steps sideways for every step forward. She reached down and scooped at my arm, hauling me up beside her. I shook myself free. I pulled out the stretched sleeve of my cardigan, eased the shape into the wool, and slid it back past my wrist. I saw the light on the still body of water, and the small muddy path that had brought us there.

"Well, you girls", Jacob said, "don't you know we came calling? Didn't you hear us?"

Well, suppose I did, I thought. Suppose she was right. I can just hear myself, can't you, bawling, here, Daddy Jack, here I am. It was seven o'clock. They had been composing sandwiches and Jacob had been for ice cream and wafers. Though missed, we had never been a crisis. The main point was that we should be there for the right food at the right time.

The little boys slept on the way home, and I suppose so did I. The next day, next week, next months are lost to me. It startles me now that I can't imagine how I said goodbye to Tabby, and that I can't even remember at what point in the evening she melted away, her crayons in her satchel and her memories in her head. Somehow, with good fortune on our side, my family must have rolled home; and it would be another few years before we ventured so far again.

Lost is not now a major capacity of mine. I don't generally have to resort to that covert shuffle whereby some women turn the map upside down to count off the junctions. They say that females can't read maps and never know where they are, but recently the Ordnance Survey has appointed its first woman director, so that particular slander loses its force. I married a man who casts a professional eye on the lie of the land, and would prefer me to direct with references to tumuli, streambeds and ancient monuments. But a finger tracing the major routes is enough for me, and I just say nervously, "We are about two miles from our turn-off or maybe, of course, we are not." They are always tearing up the contour lines, ploughing under the map, playing hell with the cartography that last year you were sold as le dernier cri . As for the moorland landscape, I have turned my back on it, knowing that it was just an accident that I was born there, that I have no affinity with its bleakness. At least one of those pinching little boys in the back seat shares my appreciation of wildflower verges and lush arable acres. And in recent years, since Jack has been wandering in the country of the dead, I see again his brown skin, his roving caramel eyes, his fretting rage against power and its abuses: and I think perhaps that he was lost all his life, and looking for a house of justice, a place of safety to take him in.

In the short term, though, we continued to live in one of those houses where there was never any money, and doors were slammed hard. One day the glass did spring out of the kitchen cupboard, at the touch of my fingertips. At once I threw my hands up, to protect my eyes. Between my fingers, for some years, you could see the delicate scars, like the ghosts of lace gloves, that the cuts left behind.

February 1, 2002

Some Time I Shall Sleep Out

J. Maclaren-Ross

The night-sergeant at the police station surveyed me dubiously from behind his desk. "Not drunk, are you?" he said.
"No. But all the hotels are full and I want a bed for the night."

"Can't book you unless you're drunk, I'm afraid", the sergeant said. "We're full up too, anyhow." He nodded towards a noise of muffled shouting from the cells. "Whitsun", he said. "Drunks. Not a single bit of room to spare. If you've any money, you might try the YMCA. Or the Salvation Army Hostel, Waterloo way."

"Crammed to the doors. I've been." "Well, there's always Euston Station. The waiting-room." He looked up at the clock; it was already 2 a.m. "Might get in there if you hurry. Course, officially, you're not supposed to sleep on the station, but chances are no constable'll bother you. Got all we can cope with here tonight."

I thanked him and wandered out into a wide empty road balefully lit by orange sodium lamps. Voices singing Mother Machree died away in the distance and traffic had temporarily ceased. I'd been walking about for hours, and my brief-case seemed by now to weigh a ton. I stood on the kerb, a sudden prey to agoraphobia, daunted by the shining width of the street I had to cross.

Then, ahead of me, I saw the lone figure of a man approaching. It bore down slowly, limping a little, with the inexorable step of some symbolic character in a foreign film: one who might turn out to be Destiny, Satan, or perhaps even the Saviour. This effect of a fated encounter was heightened by his opening address, delivered as he drew level and halted.

"Bound for Euston, I daresay?"

"Yes. Are you?"

The man nodded, looking at me sadly and with compassion. He wore a plastic mac and carried a small attaché case of considerable antiquity. He himself was not young either, though his actual age, in the lurid sodium glare, was hard to assess.

"Euston Station", he said. "The only place where one is allowed to rest in comparative peace and comfort, free of charge. Come, let us make the journey together."

He took my arm and steered me across the road towards crimson neon capitals spelling out the station's name. "Charing Cross is no good nowadays", he said. "Doesn't open till 5 a.m. I was an inmate of Rowton House until this evening but, alas, they don't let you remain more than three nights in succession – and besides I haven't the entrance-fee." He paused in the vast booking-hall to remove his shoe and shake from inside it a sizeable lump of grit. "I am an anachronism", he said. "An officer of the First World War." Swiftly he whipped from his pocket a small tin box and allowed me to glance inside. It contained medal ribbons of indubitable 14–18 vintage. "Pensioned of course, but it's not enough to live on, and frankly whenever it comes in, I blow the lot."

At a brisker pace, as though revived by the thought of this improvidence, he moved towards the doors of the waiting-room and stood alertly surveying the terrain. "Not too bad considering", he said. I followed him into what was in fact another huge hall, where every cough raised a hollow echo, and where the benches, padded in scarlet leather, were almost all occupied by sleeping people: some huddled in pairs, others – fortunate enough to secure a bench to themselves – stretched out full length with their feet up. Few had luggage, though some soldiers' heads were pillowed on their packs, and many stirred awake at the sound of our footsteps on the tiled floor.

"This way", the officer told me, heading straight in front of him. "Avoid the Russian", he added in a lower tone, indicating a bench on our right. Slumped half across this was an old man wearing several overcoats, a green furry cap pulled low over his ears, and a matted yellow-white beard. He also wore two pairs of boots, with folded newspaper inserted between their gaping toes, and muttered malevolently to himself as we approached.

"Verminous", the officer hissed in my ear, steering me towards a vacant bench at the rear, on to which he sank with a sigh. I was about to follow suit, but started suddenly back in alarm. Towering above me was a gigantic figure, sightless and square-bearded, carved out of snuff-coloured stone and clutching a scroll.

"Stephenson", the officer said. "The Rocket, you know. Gives one quite a turn, doesn't he?"

I sat uneasily below the statue and took fuller stock of my surroundings. I saw now that round the walls, at regular intervals, were a series of large black bins resembling sarcophagi, on each of which a sleeping man lay recumbent, like a figure sculpted in relief upon his own tomb. But before I'd time to comment on this sepulchral feature of the station, the officer clutched my arm.

"Police!" he hissed. "If accosted, say you're waiting for the 7.55 to Manchester. We'll be away by then."

But the two constables were not aiming to question us. They were headed for the Russian, who watched them approach with rancour, scratching first inside one of his overcoats and then in his beard. "They'll move him on for sure", the officer said. "Poor old devil." He was right, but not until a spirited exchange had taken place, during which the Russian produced masses of tattered documents, some from inside his boots, and proferred them as evidence that he was a bona fide traveller. But the police were adamant: plainly the Russian was not waiting for the 7.55 to Manchester. At last he rose and shuffled away, with the two constables pacing behind, and those who had awoken settled down to sleep again.

"Now for a spot of shut-eye", the officer said. "Until the Buffet opens, five o'clock sharp," and he dropped off immediately, sitting bolt upright with his attaché case clipped firmly between his ankles. I didn't find it easy to follow his example, my head kept slipping off the arm I attempted to rest it on, and the sleepless antiseptic glare of the light-globes beat down from above.

Nevertheless I woke to find the officer shaking me gently and pointing with his other hand towards the Refreshment Room, part of which was called the Flying Scot, and where signs of movement were now perceptible beyond the closed glass doors. "Quick", he said. "Before the lunch rush begins. That is, if you've the wherewithal, dear boy."

At that moment the door clanged open and the rush began in earnest. Even the sarcophagus-men rose from their death-like trance and flung themselves down to join in the stampede. But, owing to the officer's foresight, we were first in the queue, and soon sitting at a table well-screened from the rest of the room, with sausage-rolls, sandwiches, and cups of coffee before us.

"A welcome break", the officer said, munching avidly. "Bless you, dear boy. One day I may be able to repay. I haven't always been like this, not by any means. I had my own business once, but it went bust. Some people said I drank too much." He brushed crumbs from his grey military moustache, clipped toothbrush-style. "Malicious gossip, of course. Then I got married. Well, enough said. I daresay you've had woman-trouble yourself. Mine, to cut it short, is a sordid simple story of domestic infelicity. She had a parrot", he said with sudden venom. "A parrot and a pekinese. Also oodles of dough. But I got away from her in the end." He dozed lightly off with his head bowed over the empty plate, then awoke to say: "Freedom. I prize my freedom above all things. I'll never go back, never. On the other hand, I'm getting a bit ancient for this kind of life. Anno domini, dear boy. I was sixty-five last birthday."

At this point I dozed off myself; when I awoke, to the clatter of cups being collected, daylight had broken over the hall outside, women with mops and pails were swabbing down the tiles, and the Whitsun crowd was pushing eagerly in from the booking-hall. "Now for a wash-and-brush-up, dear fellow", the officer said, jumping up greatly refreshed.

Downstairs we washed and shaved; and afterwards, opening his attaché case, the officer took out brushes of various kinds, polished his shoes and brushed his clothes carefully, even combing his moustache with a tiny tortoise-shell comb. "I've made a decision, my boy", he said. "I'm going back. Back to the wife. It'll mean sacrificing my freedom, but against that there's my age. It's a fact one's got to admit, getting older. Oh, she'll take me in all right. I've only got to turn up. No, no, thanks – I've saved the fare all right. It's not far, on the Tube, to her suburban mansion."

We said good-bye at the Underground entrance, and I watched him walk away. Once he shivered slightly, perhaps thinking of the parrot and the pekinese, but then he pulled his shoulders back and trod jauntily out of sight: as years before, perhaps, he had led his men over the top, at zero-hour, on some forgotten field.

December 20, 2002